CW01402007

'You're not ... **picked up th** ...

'I had plans for ... didn't mention h ... home had faded as she'd struggled to keep the medical practice afloat. They'd all paid a high price for an incident out of their control.

'You betrayed me as well,' she continued.

'And just how did I do that?'

'You didn't return my calls or answer my letters. After we'd become...' She quickly revised her sentence. 'After we'd spent so much time together, how do you think I felt when you left without a goodbye and refused to speak to me again? Do you know how many nights I ached to hear the sound of your voice? How many times I apologised to you in my thoughts, hoping that with my next call I could say it for real?'

Gavin didn't answer for several long seconds. 'It was for the best,' he finally muttered.

'Oh, really? I happen to disagree.'

Jessica Matthews's interest in medicine began at a young age, and she nourished it with medical stories and hospital-based television programmes. After a stint as a teenage candy-striper, she pursued a career as a clinical laboratory scientist. When not writing or on duty she fills her day with countless family and school-related activities. Jessica lives in the central United States with her husband, daughter and son.

A DOCTOR'S HONOUR

BY
JESSICA MATTHEWS

MILLS & BOON®

MILLS & BOON and MILLS & BOON with the Rose Device are registered trademarks of the publisher.

First published in Great Britain 2002
Harlequin Mills & Boon Limited,
Eton House, 18-24 Paradise Road, Richmond, Surrey TW9 1SR

© Jessica Matthews 2002

ISBN 0 263 83088 8

Set in Times Roman 10½ on 11½ pt.
03-0902-48998

Printed and bound in Spain
by Litografía Rosés, S.A., Barcelona

CHAPTER ONE

"He's going to say no," Isabel Daniels predicted over the telephone.

Alison Crawford waved aside her receptionist's dire warning as she paced as far as the cord on her hotel phone would allow. "You don't know that for sure."

Izzie, as Isabel was affectionately called, snorted. A handsome black woman in her late forties, she had single-handedly run the Crawford Medical Practice ever since her husband had died in a truck accident five years earlier. "Nothing is for certain except death and taxes but, mark my words, girl, what Gavin Sinclair is going to tell you ranks a close third."

Part of Aly agreed with her, but she refused to dwell on those negative thoughts. "I have to try."

Izzie's voice softened. "I know, girl. I just think you're on a fool's errand."

"I appreciate your moral support," Aly said wryly.

"If Dr Sinclair says yes, then what? Your Uncle Oliver will shoot clear through the roof when he hears what you've done."

Aly could imagine the explosion. While her uncle was eager to add another physician to his private practice, he would change his tune if she recruited Gavin Sinclair. In fact, she had mixed feelings as well, considering how he'd turned his back on her. For months she'd clutched at every plausible excuse—he was busy, his only free time came at odd hours and he was too considerate to call. When she hadn't been able to justify those any longer, she'd entertained the ridiculous—he had amnesia and didn't remember

5

her. It had taken six months and a slip of his roommate's tongue before she'd acknowledged the truth. He wouldn't call.

She'd mourned the loss of her dreams as much as she'd mourned her cousin's death. It had taken another twelve months to pass into the final stage of grief—acceptance— but now the prospect of facing Gavin caused some of her hurt and anger to resurface. However, regardless of her reservations, her uncle's situation was too desperate for her not to swallow her pride and beg for his help.

In any case, the key word to her whole plan was *if*. *If* Gavin would listen to her. *If* he said yes. He wouldn't be easily persuaded, but she intended to be most convincing. "If Gavin agrees to come, Uncle Oliver will have to accept him. He won't have a choice."

"Oliver won't see it like you do," Izzie warned. "Correct me if I'm wrong, but he still blames your Dr Sinclair for Pete's death."

Aly twisted the cord around an index finger. He wasn't *her* anything, doctor or otherwise. Gavin had been a friend of her cousin, Pete. Both had intended to join Pete's father's medical practice once they'd completed their residencies, but Pete's jet-ski accident had ended the plans for an office of Oliver Crawford and Associates, along with a few of her own.

"Gavin is our last hope," she said firmly, forcing her own issues with him into the background. "Once Uncle Oliver thinks the situation through, he'll realize it, too."

"Yeah, but—Oh-mi-gosh," Izzie exclaimed. "Your uncle just drove up. Gotta go. Good luck, girl."

The dial tone sounded in Aly's ear before she could answer. She replaced the receiver and inhaled. "Thanks, Izzie," she told her reflection in the mirror. "I'll need it."

She grabbed her purse and gave herself one last inspection before she left her room. Her French braid restrained her curly, flyaway hair for the moment, her make-up covered the signs of exhaustion and worry that had plagued her ever since she'd dreamed up her scheme, and her blue suit reeked of professionalism. She'd hidden all traces of the idealistic nursing school graduate she'd been when Gavin had visited her home town. She was officially as ready as she would ever be.

Outside, the August sun shone brightly in a cloudless sky. In spite of her inner turmoil over seeing Gavin again, only one thing would make this afternoon any more perfect, she decided as she slid behind the wheel of her red convertible. If she received what she came for, if Gavin uttered a simple three-letter word. Yes.

It was one of those days from hell.

By noon, Gavin Sinclair had assisted in two code blues, heard that his year-old sport utility vehicle needed a new transmission and learned that he had not one but *two* cavities.

To add insult to injury, Alison Crawford had walked back into his life.

Gavin stared for several long seconds as the ghost from his past stopped to study the signboard near the elevator. It couldn't be her, he decided, then changed his mind as she tilted her head in the way he remembered. Did she know he was here? On this floor? On this wing?

"You were saying something about repeating the electrolytes?" Lorena Wilcox prompted. As the fortyish charge nurse who kept an eagle eye out for her patients, she'd saved more than one from over-zealous and inattentive interns.

He dragged his thoughts off Alison and focused on the patient he'd been discussing. "Continue the IV," he repeated. "Recheck his electrolytes at four o'clock."

Lorena acknowledged the order with a brisk no-nonsense nod. "Shall I page you with the results?"

"Yes." He scribbled his orders on the chart, but his curiosity over Aly's presence rose once again.

Why was she here?

He hadn't talked to her or anyone else in her family since Peter had died. Then again, he was partly to blame for the lack of contact. After Pete's father, Oliver Crawford, had held him responsible for the accident and vocalized his feelings before God and the entire community, Gavin had shaken Hartwell's dust off his feet immediately after the funeral service. Alison had left messages during the subsequent months, but he'd never returned her calls. At first, he'd been too angered by her betrayal. Later, it had seemed pointless to keep in touch when that chapter of his life had ended.

Approaching Alison now would only stir what was better left forgotten. No doubt she'd be just as startled to see him as he was to see her.

Life was certainly full of strange coincidences.

Out of the corner of his eye he saw her approach, but he continued to write.

"Dr Sinclair?"

Gavin hesitated for a fraction of a second before he signed his name. Her voice hadn't changed. It still held a soothing, musical quality, although now he detected a discordant note of uncertainty. He closed the chart and replaced the pen in his pocket.

"Aren't you being rather formal, Alison?" He met her gaze as he purposely tacked on her name. If her intent had been to catch him off guard, she hadn't succeeded. He'd known her identity the moment she'd stepped out of the elevator.

Wariness appeared in her hazel eyes. "Considering our

surroundings and everything that's happened, I thought it more fitting.''

No doubt she was referring to the way he'd ignored her for months after Pete's death. His actions had been totally opposite from those during that fateful two-week visit. Because she'd been Pete's cousin, he'd spent a fair amount of time with her and they'd passed many happy hours together. Those occasions had only reinforced his decision to join the Crawford medical group where Aly, who had just completed her nurse's training, also worked. Between the prospect of a growing practice and a budding romantic relationship, he'd hoped the next three years would pass quickly.

They had, but not for the same reasons. Work had occupied his time and his thoughts, not dreams of a bright future with Aly at his side.

She was right. Addressing him by his title instead of using the familiarity of his name was appropriate.

''I've been all over the hospital,'' she said in an apparent attempt to change the subject. ''You're a hard man to find.''

''You just have to know where to look.''

''I guess so.'' She paused. ''You're looking well.''

''So are you.'' In fact, she looked better than he remembered. Her skin was tanned but not overly so, and the few freckles he'd considered so endearing hadn't faded on her elfin nose. Her hair was the same, too—thick dark brown tresses that had a tendency to go their own way no matter what she did. From the length of her French braid, those smooth strands now hung well past her shoulders.

As she stood before him within arm's reach, he realized how easily she fit under his chin. She'd always had a trim, athletic form, but obviously time had dimmed his memory because he didn't recall her curves being quite so lush. Then again, he'd usually seen her in oversized T-shirts and baggy shorts, not in tailored jackets and tight-fitting skirts. She'd probably worn something similar to the funeral service, but at the time he'd been too frozen with grief to notice.

Blue was certainly her color.

This train of thought led nowhere, he realized, and he hardened his resolve to maintain an emotional distance. For the first six months after Pete's accident, he'd worked to the exclusion of all else in order to drive her and his image of what might have been out of his head. As a result, he'd successfully buried the past—and the guilt—and he didn't want to unearth either one.

He watched her fingers toy with the shoulder strap of her bag. Clearly, she wasn't as cool, calm and collected as she tried to portray but, then, neither was he. He should have tried to make this easier on her, but her presence was too disturbing to his peace of mind. When Oliver had taken his grief out on Gavin, Gavin had expected Alison to stand by him. Instead, her loyalties had lain elsewhere.

Once again, ranks had closed, leaving him on the outside, looking in.

Gavin steeled himself against the memory and crossed his arms. "If you want to see someone in particular—"

"I was looking for you."

Her comment caught him by surprise, but he rapidly recovered. After he'd made a point to steer clear of her and her family, he doubted if she'd tracked him down to simply renew their acquaintance. "I'm sure you're not here on a social visit, so let's cut through the pleasantries and get to the point. I'm on a tight schedule."

He'd almost expected her to wilt under his brusque tone, but instead she squared her shoulders and raised her chin. Her eyes seemed to cool and she matched his unwavering gaze. Apparently she didn't scare as easily as she had three years ago. Pollyanna had acquired a backbone.

"I'm here because I need your help."

He raised an eyebrow. "Oh?"

Her breasts heaved as she inhaled. "Actually, it's not me. It's Uncle Oliver. He needs you."

The notion was too inconceivable for belief. The man who'd blamed him for Pete's death and who'd told him to stay away from his entire family was now asking for him? How interesting. How totally out of character. How ironic.

Gavin snorted. "I can't imagine why."

"He's sick."

"I'll give you the names of several excellent physicians." He grabbed several folders off the counter and took two steps toward the stairwell.

Alison moved in front of him. Her attempt to block his exit was farcical considering he outweighed her by at least eighty pounds. "You don't understand."

"No," he admitted. "Nor do I want to."

"Please. Listen to me before you walk away."

He started to shake his head but she placed a hand on his wrist. "You owe me this."

The truth in her accusation forced his ready refusal to die unspoken. For more reasons than he cared to count, he did owe her an opportunity for explanations. If that fact wasn't enough to soften his harsh stance, experiencing her feather-light touch and inhaling her vanilla scent after trying to forget those exact memories utterly destroyed his will-power. He would reluctantly yield to her request, but he wasn't certain of who angered him the most for his decision—Alison for reviving his dormant feelings, or himself for going against his better judgement.

"There's a waiting room at the end of this corridor. It's usually empty at this time of day, so if you're looking for privacy, it's the closest you'll get."

He could have found an office, perhaps even the same office he'd used when he'd gone to interviews with recruiters from other medical practices, but seeing her had dredged up too much of the emotion he'd successfully suppressed. To keep those feelings in check, he needed the impersonal atmosphere of a public place.

"OK."

"I'm only agreeing to hear what you have to say," he warned. "Don't read anything more into it than that."

"I won't."

She spoke as if she'd delivered a promise, but he knew better than to believe she meant what she'd said. He'd become a master at deciphering people's expressions and Alison's had definitely reflected expectancy...and hope. Dashing those same hopes would no doubt make him appear—and feel—like a first-class bum, but she might as well learn that life rarely worked out the way one planned or even wished.

Who better to teach her than a man who'd graduated at the top of his class in the School of Disappointments?

He'd grown hard...and cynical.

Alison hadn't expected Gavin to have changed so much since their days together. When she'd first met him in Hartwell, he'd been quiet, almost aloof, but after hanging around her relatives for nearly two weeks, he'd thawed to a certain degree. Now his jaw was set and the easy smile she remembered hadn't appeared at all. His slate-gray eyes were as dark as a winter sky before a storm and his voice was colder than dry ice.

Gavin obviously still harbored resentment over the way her family had treated him after the accident, and rightfully so. However, understanding his pain only partially soothed the hurts he'd inflicted on her. Although her anger had faded over the years, if she'd found another solution to her uncle's dilemma, she would have seized it with both hands.

Instead, desperation and her own conscience had convinced her to rise above her pride and attempt the impossible.

In any case, she needed to stay calm and be extremely persuasive if she wanted him to agree to her proposition. What person in his right mind would go where he thought he wasn't wanted? Which, she thought wryly, said a lot for herself.

Aly caught him staring at her and realized that her hand hadn't left his arm. She slowly broke contact and tried to ignore the tingling in her fingertips. It became a bitter-sweet revelation to realize how time and events hadn't diminished her attraction or tempered her response.

''The waiting room will be fine,'' she said as she grabbed her shoulder strap and forced herself not to dwell on the strength he exuded. He was the only man who had ever turned her insides to jelly and made her skin feel as if electricity danced across her nerve endings. She wondered how he'd react if he knew of her vulnerability, but sharing the information was out of the question. After swallowing his rejection two years ago, it would be totally humiliating if he so much as suspected her weakness.

Steeling her expression to appear as aloof as he did, she soaked up his appearance like a thirsty sponge. With an unbuttoned white coat covering a green shirt and sharply pressed black trousers, he was a sight to behold. It wasn't any wonder that no other man had caught her fancy. Then again, she hadn't had the time or the energy for a brief fling, much less a long-term romance.

As handsome as he was, he probably attracted more than his fair share of female attention. Ash-blond hair, aristocratic features and an athletic form honed by what had to be faithful exercise were combined in perfect proportions. Any woman with an ounce of estrogen flowing through her veins could dream of him without the slightest bit of effort.

As he headed in another direction, she hurried to keep

up with his long-legged stride. He obviously hadn't noticed her higher-than-usual pumps or how her slim-fitting skirt dictated the length of her own steps. Then again, perhaps he simply didn't care. In any event, it didn't matter. Gavin had agreed to listen to what she had to say.

''How's your mother?'' he asked without preamble.

So he wasn't as totally disinterested as he appeared, she thought. Taking his question as a good sign, she cheerfully answered.

''She's fine. Mom has taken on a new interest.''

''Other than painting?''

One morning, Aly had shown Gavin her mother's studio where Maggie Crawford dabbled in her oils. Her mother's talent had impressed Gavin, but one work in particular had repeatedly drawn his attention. The canvas depicted an abandoned barn, a broken windmill and a clump of wild-flowers underneath a sky filled with stormclouds and what looked like the beginnings of a tornado funnel. Those elements weren't particularly unusual, but somehow the emotion of Nature's fury shone through. A variety of sentiments, from anticipation and fear to a hope for a better tomorrow, were captured in that one moment of time, making this painting Aly's favorite. The fact that the scene had obviously stirred something inside Gavin as well had made it even more special.

She'd later squirreled the canvas away in her closet, intending to hang it in Gavin's office as a gift, but an office in Hartwell had never materialized.

For reasons she never cared to think about too deeply, she'd framed and hung the painting in her bedroom after he'd left town. If her mother had ever wondered as to the whereabouts of that specific piece, she'd never asked and Aly had never volunteered the information.

Aly smiled as she mentally pictured her vivacious but flighty parent. ''She still indulges her artistic streak, but I was actually referring to her interest in grandkids. Thanks to my oldest brother, she has three to spoil. All under the age of four.''

"What about you?"

She knew what he was asking but skirted the question. She wasn't about to admit how a love life was the furthest thing from her mind at this point. "I'm not ready for grandchildren.''

He raised his eyebrow at her and this time she thought the corners of his mouth twitched with humor. "No husband and no kids means I have plenty of time and energy to spoil my niece and nephews. That's what aunts are for.''

"I wouldn't know." He sounded distant as his gaze moved away from her to directly ahead.

She bit her lip and focused on the carpet's pattern. She'd forgotten the nutshell history Pete had given in response to her unending questions. Born to wealthy parents who'd subsequently divorced when he was young, Gavin had spent most of his time with a succession of nannies who'd eventually been replaced with boarding schools. It wasn't any wonder that he had no idea how a family operated.

Stealing a glance at him, she noted his bare fingers as they curled around the folders. Curiosity wouldn't be denied, although as soon as she spoke, she wanted to recall her question. Why be a glutton for punishment? "Is there a *Mrs* Dr Sinclair, or one waiting in the wings?''

"No.''

A wave of relief flooded over her. She told herself it was only because his single status might make him more receptive to her proposition if he didn't have a wife or a fiancée in tow. It had nothing to do with her own joy that the woman she'd learned about several years ago had disappeared from the scene.

Aly followed him into a large corner room which stood empty, as predicted. He motioned her to a round table with four chairs while he stopped in front of a vending machine. She rummaged in her purse for spare change to buy a drink, not because she was thirsty but because holding a can would keep her hands busy.

It was as if he'd read her mind. Before she could locate four quarters, he returned with two cold bottles of non-carbonated water. The fragrance of sandalwood-scented soap drifted in her direction as he sat next to her and her thoughts scattered like dandelion seeds in a stiff breeze.

"Thanks," she said, unscrewing the lid to take a dainty sip. After watching him follow suit, she knew her momentary reprieve had ended. With any luck, those hours of practicing her speech would pay off and he would be so moved by her story that he couldn't possibly refuse her.

Gavin leaned back and crossed his arms. "So you think you need my help."

"I *know* we need your help. Uncle Oliver can't handle the practice by himself any longer."

"If I recall, he's not the only doctor in town."

"No, but the others are getting older, too. One has already retired and the other won't accept any new patients."

"So hire someone to take over for your uncle."

"He's tried. In the last year, *I've* tried. I haven't found any takers."

"Oliver is stubborn. He'll manage."

"No, he won't," she insisted. "Between his arthritis and his diabetes, he's simply not able to cope with the physical demands. We've had to call in a locum three times in the last twelve months."

He shrugged. "Maybe one of those guys would be interested in the practice."

She shook her head. "I've already asked. They don't mind staying a few weeks in Hartwell, but no one is interested in a long-term arrangement. Everyone wants regular time off, including weekends, and with limited medical backup we just can't give that guarantee. And if that detail doesn't turn them away, the idea of covering the hospital's emergency room, in addition to their private patient caseload, does.''

"So hire an ER physician."

"We would if we could justify the expense. Unfortunately, our ER isn't extremely busy, but one case can take several hours out of an evening. A steady diet of that schedule doesn't appeal to physicians. We're in a vicious circle.''

"I sympathize, but I don't see how I can help other than by giving you a few leads."

She drew a deep breath and leaned closer. "I didn't come to ask for more names."

His eyes narrowed. "Then what *are* you here for?"

"To ask you to join my uncle's practice."

The words were finally out. She'd expected him to be shocked and he hadn't failed her. He froze before her eyes and the seconds stretched interminably as she waited for a response.

Suddenly, his eyes crinkled and he laughed, the sound more scornful than cheery. "You're expecting me to do what no one else will? You've got to be joking."

"No, I'm not," she said solemnly.

His expression became one of incredulity. "You really are serious, aren't you?"

"Yes."

Gavin leaned forward to reach for his bottle of water. Hearing the hum of the vending machines in the background, she watched his throat work as he swallowed. His motions were clearly a stalling tactic while he considered her request. She clutched her hands together in silent supplication underneath the table. He couldn't refuse. He simply couldn't!

"Even if I considered such a crazy idea—which I am

not I might add—what made you think of me?'' he asked some moments later. ''We haven't kept in touch. Why wait until now to drop by?''

Aly thought she'd worked through her anger long ago, but obviously it had been simmering all this time because now it boiled over. ''Why wait until now?'' she echoed. ''That's a rich statement, coming from you. Need I spell out how I *tried* to stay in touch? Shall I describe in detail how *you* were the one who treated me as if I carried a contagious disease?''

His eyes widened, as if he hadn't expected her to go on the offensive. ''So don't blame me for our loss of contact,'' she warned him indignantly. ''I may have been a slow learner three years ago, but I did eventually get the picture.''

To be honest, in her weaker moments she'd considered talking to Gavin in person rather than over the phone, but she hadn't possessed enough courage to do so. It was one thing to experience rejection long distance and quite another to meet it face to face. Now, however, she had him speechless and she couldn't stop from pouring out her thoughts.

''I wouldn't have come now,'' she added stiffly, ''if it weren't for Uncle Oliver's situation. He was in the hospital a month ago for pneumonia and during that week I managed his business affairs. When I went through his files, I stumbled across a letter you'd written two years ago.''

Something flashed in his eyes before it disappeared. ''I'm surprised he kept it.''

As she'd read those two short paragraphs she'd been surprised, too, before she'd become intrigued, excited and full of hope for the first time since the day she'd accepted that Gavin was part of her past and not her future. The reasons why her uncle had kept that particular sheet of correspondence eluded her, but she hadn't questioned him. Instead, she'd taken matters into her own hands.

"As I read the letter, I couldn't believe that you were willing to work in Hartwell as you'd originally agreed. Not after the things Uncle Oliver had said…"

"You mean, after he nearly ran me out of town?"

Her skin warmed with embarrassment. "Yes."

He shrugged. "For all I knew, Oliver had calmed down and still wanted a partner. Not wanting to make any assumptions one way or another, I felt obligated to check with him before I started looking elsewhere. Physicians are recruited long before they actually finish training, you know."

She knew full well when and how quickly doctors found positions. Those who were available to enter private practice were already under contract and had been for some time. For Gavin to contact her uncle when he'd probably had a good idea of the outcome spoke highly of his integrity. "Did he ever answer?"

He snorted. "I'll say. Something along the lines of 'when hell freezes over'. I'm surprised you didn't find a copy of *that* letter in his files." He paused. "So now he's had a change of heart?"

Once again she skirted the question. "He's desperate for another physician. After I found your letter, I forced the issue and here I am." She crossed her fingers. Although she hadn't told a lie, she'd omitted a lot of details that would guarantee Gavin's refusal if she shared them.

"And I'm supposed to come running because of something I wrote two years ago?"

She met his gaze. "We're in dire straits, Gavin."

"Well, I'm not. I'm committed elsewhere."

"Surely you can change your mind."

"I could, but I won't. I don't go back on my word."

"If you won't do it for Uncle Oliver, do it for Pete,"

she urged as she fought down her rising panic. "You made your promise to him first."

He waved his hands. "Oh, no. You can't lay a guilt trip on me. I tried to pay my debt, to honor my commitment. Your uncle refused my offer, which absolves me of any moral responsibility."

"Haven't you ever said or done anything impulsively?" she asked, thinking of her uncle's outburst. "Something you regretted later, but didn't know how to rectify?"

"Not since I was thirteen."

What could she say to make him reconsider? Her thoughts raced but the only words forming were the only words she'd wanted to tell him over the phone. If he sent her packing, at least she would go back knowing he'd finally heard her apology. It probably wouldn't make any difference, but she had to try.

"You never gave me the opportunity to tell you how sorry I was for everything that happened and for everything that didn't." After touching the sore spot of a subject, she couldn't stop until she'd unburdened herself. "I should have stuck by you when Uncle Oliver created his scene. You didn't deserve being treated so harshly and I understand how betrayed you must have felt. All I can say is that, like everyone else, I was devastated by Pete's death and shocked at my uncle's loss of control."

As long as she lived, she would never forget her uncle's breakdown. How he'd turned on Gavin and poured out his anger over the loss of his son on his son's best friend. To her utmost regret, she had stood by and said nothing. Even when Gavin had looked to her for support, she'd urged him to go, as her uncle had demanded. Unfortunately, her attempt to keep peace until cooler heads prevailed had failed.

"Although in my own defense, I didn't expect you to leave town or disappear completely from my life. I thought you'd just leave the cemetery."

"Why stay where I wasn't wanted? Anyway, it's ancient history. Forget it." In spite of Gavin's casual attitude, Aly sensed that he hadn't forgotten. Just as she hadn't.

"I *can't* forget it," she said vehemently. "I've tried. I doubt if you've completely forgotten the incident either. You've only buried the hurt but the pain hasn't gone away."

"So you're a counselor now?"

She ignored his sarcastic tone as she allowed a chilly note in her voice. "No, but I've had to cope with the aftermath just as you have. You aren't the only one who's picked up the pieces and gone on. I had plans for my life, too, you know." She didn't mention the specifics of how her dreams of hearth and home had faded as she'd struggled to keep Oliver's medical practice afloat. They'd all paid a high price for an incident out of their control.

"And if you want to get technical," she continued, "you betrayed me as well."

"And just how did I do that?"

"You didn't return my calls or answer my letters. After we'd become…" She quickly revised her sentence. "After we'd spent so much time together, how do you think I felt when you left without a goodbye and refused to speak to me again? Do you know how many nights I ached to hear the sound of your voice? How many times I apologized to you in my thoughts, hoping that with my next call I could say it for real?"

Gavin didn't answer for several long seconds. "It was for the best," he finally muttered.

She swallowed the knot growing in her throat, hating that he'd seen the hurt he'd inflicted, the same hurt that she'd vowed not to show him, the same hurt that she'd thought she'd put behind her. "Oh, really? I happen to disagree."

His slate-colored eyes grew dark. "Do *you* believe I was responsible for Pete's death?"

"No," Aly answered instantly. "You did everything you could to save his life. I don't think I've ever seen anyone work as hard and as long as you did. But even if you had been able to resuscitate him, the pathologist said it was difficult to say what quality of life he would have had with his head injuries. It was an accident, a trick of fate. If anything, it was Pete's fault for being inattentive. He should have been watching where he was going."

Gavin fell silent, and when he eventually spoke his voice sounded far away as if he were reliving that fateful day. "We should have golfed or played tennis instead. Did you know Oliver had asked us to go fishing?"

"Yes," she said gently. "But Pete hated to sit still. The outing was his decision and he was too strong-willed for anyone to convince him otherwise."

"What does the rest of your family think?"

"They agree with me." Her mother and her brothers all shared her belief. Her uncle was the only one who insisted on Gavin's culpability, but she wasn't about to share his opinion on the matter. Gavin would never think twice about her offer if he even *suspected* that Oliver wasn't one hundred per cent in favor of his return. Because she'd vowed to take one step at a time, she'd work on Oliver's attitude once she'd enlisted Gavin. There wasn't any point in fighting a battle before its time.

"But now you want me to come to Hartwell."

Actually, she was torn between wanting him there and wanting him to stay away. For her uncle's sake, she would swallow her own hurts and disillusionment.

"We need you," she answered simply. "You'll have the same terms as before."

"Why isn't Oliver asking me this?"

She'd hoped the question wouldn't come up but since it had, she repeated the half-truths she'd practiced for this eventuality. With luck, she would sound convincing.

"Someone has to mind the store. And, to be honest, I thought I had a better chance of persuading you."

He nodded. Apparently he accepted her explanation, which let her breathe a little easier for the moment. "Can't you hire a physician's assistant? A PA would cut Oliver's load considerably."

"We—I—tried, but no one was interested. People with those qualifications need to practice under the supervision of a licensed physician and with Oliver's health problems they might be out of work before long. I can't blame them for their decision. No one is eager to wind up in the unemployment line at a moment's notice. They want job security as much as the next guy.

"It seemed more logical to go back to school than to waste my time looking for someone." At his questioning glance, she explained. "I recently passed my nurse-practitioner exams. I can officially take some of the burden off his shoulders, but you know as well as I do that a lot of procedures can only be performed by a doctor."

Gavin's chair scraped the linoleum as he rose. "I see the dilemma you're in, but I'm sorry. I can't help you. I'm not your man."

She rose, too. "You could be."

He shook his head. "It wouldn't work."

"What would it take to convince you?" She hated the note of desperation in her voice, but she couldn't filter it out.

"Nothing. I have commitments of my own."

"I heard you're moving into a practice with five other doctors. Surely they could spare you..."

"Probably," he agreed, "*if* I truly wanted to back out, but I don't."

Aly was determined to change his mind. "Uncle Oliver should close his office, but he refuses to leave his patients without a successor." She didn't mention the issue concerning her most—his precarious mental state. He didn't have the zest for living that he'd once had, and she was certain his attitude played a huge role in why he didn't watch his blood sugar as well as he should. Granted, he was doing better than he had been six months ago, but it was only because she hounded him at every turn.

"I can't solve your problem. You'll have to get someone else." He moved away from the table and she intercepted him.

"Did I tell you what happened six months ago? I found him unconscious. His glucose was over five hundred. The next time I find him…" She left that scenario to his imagination.

"I can't help you."

His dispassionate tone made her angry. "This is all about revenge, isn't it?"

He turned to face her. "No. Your uncle refused my offer and so I made other plans. Case closed."

She wasn't convinced by his answer. His reply came too quickly and sounded too well practiced. She should have dropped the subject, but she couldn't contain her frustration. "You've changed."

He snorted. "People do. I'm simply looking out for myself."

"And the heck with everybody else?"

"Yes."

"I see." She paused. "Do you hate us that much?"

"If you must know, I don't feel a thing."

His comment shouldn't have hurt her, but it did. "Fine," she said stiffly as she squared her shoulders. "I'm sorry I took up your time. *Doctor*."

She turned away to retrieve her purse off the table, her heels muffled by the carpeting. Tears would come later, but for now she found solace in cool, emotional distance.

"How long will you be in town?"

She slung her purse over her shoulder. Intent on leaving him behind in her rush for the exit, she asked, "Why do you care?"

Gavin lifted his wide shoulders in a careless shrug. "I might think of a few people who'd be interested..."

"Don't bother."

He caught her arm as she walked past. "You asked for my help."

"Not the kind you're offering."

Aly yanked herself free and continued on her way. Her failure tasted bitter, especially when she imagined how her uncle would brush aside her warnings to slow down and take care of himself.

Gavin had seemed to be the perfect solution to their problem, but obviously she'd pinned her hopes on the wrong man. Perhaps if she approached the family medicine department, they could point her in the direction of other candidates.

What if they *aren't interested either?*

Maybe she should let Gavin make enquiries. His network was sure to be larger and more effective than hers. What would it hurt? Her whole purpose in coming to Oklahoma City had been to recruit a physician. Gavin might have been the only doctor with whom she had some leverage, but he wasn't the only doctor in town.

Before she could talk herself out of her sudden change of heart, she turned to see Gavin standing where she'd left him. "I'm at the Holiday Inn. Room 340. I'll be leaving the day after tomorrow."

He nodded. "I'll do what I can."

Aly didn't answer. She *couldn't* answer. Although she'd heard plenty of refusals during the course of her search, none had bothered her as much as his did. Yet it was her fault. She knew better than to let personal feelings get entangled in a business proposition, but she'd done it anyway.

Although she knew the chances had been slim to none, she'd still carried the faintest of hopes that the differences between Gavin, her uncle and herself could be reconciled. During her more fanciful moments, she'd envisioned undoing the damage she'd caused this man who'd slipped into her heart with amazing ease. In turn, her own wounds would have been healed.

In reality, she hadn't been successful. If only she'd done things differently three years ago... Unfortunately, she hadn't, and there wasn't any sense in bemoaning what couldn't be changed.

Time was supposed to heal all wounds, but in her case it had made them strangers.

CHAPTER TWO

HE HADN'T been totally honest.

"Aw, hell," Gavin muttered under his breath. He'd lied through his teeth. Telling Alison that he didn't feel anything for her or her family had only been a defensive maneuver. Even now, he wouldn't admit how much Oliver Crawford's diatribe had stung.

What had hurt far worse, however, had been the way Aly had defended her uncle and encouraged Gavin to give them all time to deal with their loss. Hadn't they realized how his loss had equaled theirs? Hadn't they considered that Pete had been the brother he'd always wanted? He'd thought Aly had known, but clearly he'd been mistaken. With Pete gone, he refused to endure the same push-pull relationship with the Crawfords that he'd tolerated for so many years with his parents—welcomed only when his presence had been convenient. This time, *he* was in control.

Three years ago, the combination of his attraction to Aly and the bond of a mutual professional vision for the community had made a match between them seemed preordained. No matter how easily that same attraction might ignite now, he knew better than to dream of or expect a happy ending.

This is all about revenge, isn't it?

Little did Alison know how wrong she was. How could he want revenge against a man for speaking the truth?

As soon as nearby boaters had hauled Pete to shore, Gavin had started CPR. His friend's injuries had been severe, but Gavin had dealt with traumas during his stint in the ER. He'd known exactly what to do—open the airway,

27

restore breathing and maintain circulation—and he did it as he had many other times. Unfortunately, on this particular occasion, when he'd wanted a successful outcome more than he'd ever wanted it before, he'd failed.

Oliver had had every right to blame Gavin for the things he'd lost, because Gavin had blamed himself. He'd owed everyone, from Pete's family to the entire community, for their loss of a beloved son and physician. He'd wanted to pay his debt and find closure in the process, but Oliver had refused him the opportunity. In the end, Gavin had found solace in his studies and had moved on with his life.

Revenge? Not a chance.

He also realized with some chagrin how he'd treated Aly, both today and in the past, with the same degree of cold-heartedness Oliver had shown him. He should have let her down gently, instead of treating her as a pariah, but he hadn't. For what it was worth, he'd add these incidents to his list of regrets. But at least she wouldn't cling to un-warranted hopes.

Unfortunately, she would never believe that his refusal had nothing to do with the past and everything to do with the opportunities awaiting him at the top internal medicine practice in the state. Neither would she believe that saying no had been far harder than he'd made it sound.

Oliver needed Gavin if Aly's story was true, but he wasn't totally convinced that the older man *wanted* him. Even if Oliver couldn't extend his offer in person, a phone call or letter would have gone a long way to ease Gavin's misgivings. Oliver may have possessed an excessive amount of pride, but Gavin had a fair amount of his own as well.

It was better—safer—to help the Crawfords by finding someone other than himself to step into the gap. That way, their need would be met and his guilt would finally be assuaged.

He strolled to the residents-only lounge and began making phone calls, using his mental list of colleagues. It didn't take long to realize that he couldn't honor his promise to Aly. He couldn't supply her with a single prospect because every suitable physician was committed elsewhere.

Aw, Pete. Why did you have to be so reckless?

The guilt he'd held at bay for three long years grew stronger. It doubled as he pictured Aly finding Oliver lying unconscious on the floor and again as he recalled the drawn look on her face and the faint dark circles under her eyes. The last few years had obviously had been tough on her.

While he sympathized, giving up his position with the prestigious Upton Medical Group for a small-town practice in the panhandle seemed foolhardy, if not downright crazy.

His decision shouldn't have been difficult, but it was. While both of his opportunities presented unique challenges, the problem lay in determining which challenge he wanted more.

His pager demanded his attention. The number on the display connected him directly to Lorena.

"A new admission," she reported. "ER is sending you a fifty-year-old male with abdominal pain and fatigue. His initial CBC shows a WBC of two thousand and ninety-five per cent lymphocytes."

With the low white count and increased lymphs, one diagnosis came to mind immediately. "ALL?" he asked, using the abbreviation for acute lymphocytic leukemia.

"That's what the folks in ER suspect," she said.

"So why didn't they send him to Oncology instead of Internal Medicine?"

"He specifically asked for Dr Townsend."

The request was made more often than not. Townsend was notorious for giving personal attention to his patients and, as his resident, Gavin had seen the fierce loyalty those same patients displayed toward the older physician. As for

himself, he couldn't have asked to work under a finer man
or to have a better role model. "Did you call him?"

"The ER staff did. He's coming in later and said he'd
talk to you about this guy then."

"Fine. I'll be right there."

Gavin arrived at the nurses' station within three minutes.
In no time at all, he'd reviewed the results of the preliminary tests the ER staff had ordered.

In addition to the reported history of unusual bruising,
fatigue and night sweats, Gavin's physical examination
gave him other troubling information. He'd discovered enlarged lymph nodes in both the patient's groin and under
his arm, as well as an enlarged spleen.

"I'd like to schedule you for a bone marrow tomorrow,
Reverend Lodge," Gavin told the frail-looking man in the
hospital bed.

"A bone marrow?" The reverend glanced at his wife.
"Isn't that a test for leukemia?"

"Yes, but we can determine a variety of other conditions
from the test as well."

Mrs Lodge gasped and her face crumpled as she fought
back tears.

"So you think that's what's wrong with me?"

Gavin hated this part of being a doctor. "It's a possibility. Your symptoms point in that direction."

Lodge glanced at his wife, then back again at Gavin.
"How long does it take to find out?"

"A few days," Gavin answered. "If the pathologist sees
abnormal cells, he'll call me right away. Then we'll schedule you for an oncology appointment."

"If it's not leukemia?"

"Then we'll either treat the problem or refer you to a
specialist who can." Gavin thought it highly unlikely to be
any other condition, but he didn't want to destroy the man's
hopes. After all, he could be wrong.

"You're the boss," Lodge said.

"As soon as I schedule your procedure with the lab, I'll let you know. In the meantime, try to rest. Any questions?"

As he'd expected, both husband and wife shook their heads. The shock hadn't worn off yet, but when it did they would have plenty of things to ask.

Gavin headed for the door. "Dr Townsend will drop in on you later. Otherwise, I'll see you in the morning."

By the time he'd taken care of all the paperwork and arranged for the bone marrow with the pathology staff, Conrad Townsend had arrived. "How's Norm?" he asked in his usual booming voice. In his youth, some thirty-five years earlier, he'd played football and still had the body to match. "He's the minister of my church, you know."

Gavin hadn't, but he understood Townsend's genuine concern for all of his patients, even if his residents were responsible for their care. "It may be leukemia."

Townsend sighed. "I was afraid of that. He hasn't looked good these past few weeks. Still, if something else is the cause, you'll find it."

"Thanks." During the past two years, Townsend had delighted in passing his most difficult cases to Gavin and Gavin hadn't failed him. Then again, it shouldn't have come as any surprise. Gavin spent most of his free time poring over the literature in search of answers. Most of his resident colleagues didn't approach a problem with the same tenacity, and their success rates weren't as high.

"I've scheduled a bone marrow in the morning," Gavin added. "Do you want to do the honors?"

"Go ahead. I'll just drop in on Norm and reassure him that he's in good hands." He turned to leave, then paused. "It won't be long until you join Upton's group. I'll bet you can't wait."

"It will be nice to be on my own," he said slowly.

"It is at that," Townsend agreed. "You're fortunate to

have landed such a prestigious position so early in your career. It takes most physicians years to get where you're starting.''

''I'm very lucky,'' Gavin admitted.

''That's not to say you don't deserve it. You've definitely earned your spot. And yet I don't envy you.''

Gavin didn't understand. ''Sir?''

''I started in a two-physician clinic and loved every minute. Granted, I had to keep up with a larger variety of treatments and diseases than I did when I specialized, but knowing the people who came to me—*really* knowing them—was wonderful.''

''Why didn't you stay there?''

''My wife's parents developed health problems and she wanted to be close enough to keep tabs on them, so we ended up here in the city.''

''Would you make the same choices if you could do it over again?''

''Of course. I really enjoy my work here,'' Townsend hastened to add. ''My career has been extremely rewarding, especially when I think about all the doctors I've influenced. Why do you ask?''

''I've been approached to go to a small practice in Hartwell.''

''Ah, yes. Didn't you have plans to go there at one time?''

Gavin nodded.

Townsend pursed his mouth in a thoughtful line, as if he was puzzled by his star resident's sudden change of heart. ''I wouldn't presume to tell you what to do, but my advice is to go wherever you'll be the most satisfied. Only you know where that will be. If you pass up Upton's opportunity, make sure you do it for the right reasons.''

Townsend's counsel was sound, but it didn't help Gavin resolve his dilemma. He mulled over their conversation as he sat behind the nurses' counter with the latest *New England Journal of Medicine* in hand and stared at the table of contents. The first article listed was a study on the latest form of insulin, and naturally his thoughts turned to Aly and her uncle.

If he chose to return to Hartwell, what *was* his rationale? Was it feasible to complete the plans he and Pete had made now that Pete wasn't part of the equation?

"This is a switch," Lorena commented.

He glanced up and smiled at the woman who acted as mother hen to all of the unit's staff, regardless of their position. If they were younger than she was—and most were—she dispensed whatever the situation called for, whether it was encouragement, sympathy or correction. She had a gift for saying the right thing at the right time, and everyone usually breathed easier when she reported for duty.

"What is?" he asked.

"You've been staring at the same page for the last five minutes. You normally would be through half a magazine in that length of time and could summarize everything you've read to boot."

"You're exaggerating."

"Only a little. Things are slow. Why don't you go home?"

"I will. My shift ends in twenty minutes."

"Lucky you." The phone rang and she turned away to answer it.

Gavin flipped to the diabetes article and tried to read. Fortunately, John Mason, his fellow third-year resident, arrived at that moment, looking less than his usual perky self.

Gavin studied him. "Having had a four-day vacation, you don't look too rested and relaxed."

John groaned. "Don't remind me."

Lorena finished her phone conversation and joined in. "Too much partying, no doubt."

"It wasn't partying in the true sense of the word, although Becky and I didn't get much sleep. Making up for lost time, you know." He wiggled his eyebrows.

Life as a resident wasn't conducive to maintaining a romance, at least not in Gavin's opinion. Probably not in Becky's either.

"When *are* you going to stop stringing that girl along and tie the knot?" Lorena chided.

John shrugged. "We have plenty of time. Besides, she doesn't want to move to Georgia. Says it's too hot and muggy there."

"Most accountants don't work outdoors," Gavin pointed out. He knew Becky's profession because he'd celebrated with them when she'd passed her certified public accountant's exam.

"Yeah, I know. Go figure."

John had talked about returning to his home state ever since they'd started their residencies. John had filled Pete's unexpectedly vacant spot, and so their first weeks together had been difficult because he'd been a constant reminder of Pete's death. Thanks to John's tenacity and good humor, though, they'd eventually become friends. While they weren't as close as he and Pete had been, they were buddies nevertheless.

"Speaking of moving," Gavin said, "have either of you heard of anyone who's looking for a small-town general practice?"

Lorena appeared thoughtful and John shook his head.

Gavin hadn't expected them to mention any names that he hadn't already considered, but he had to try. "Well, if you do, let me know. Preferably today."

John whistled. "What's the rush?"

"There's a doctor in Hartwell who needs someone to

step into his practice right away. The person to talk to is only in town until Wednesday.''

''The chances of him finding anyone are slim to none,'' John warned. ''Most of us made our choices long ago.''

''I know, but I have to try.''

John straddled a nearby chair. ''What gives? Why are *you* suddenly Robbie Recruiter?''

Unwilling to explain his reasons, Gavin shrugged. ''An Alison Crawford is searching for a doctor. I told her I'd see what I could do.''

''Hartwell. Crawford.'' John tapped his temple. ''Why do those names sound familiar?'' Suddenly he snapped his fingers. ''I remember now. You were going to go there. And isn't she the one who always phoned and I had to cover for you?''

Avoiding her seemed so childish now. ''Yeah.''

''Well, why don't you sign up for their opening?''

''I've agreed to join Upton's clinic.''

''Agreements are made to be broken.''

''Mine aren't.''

''Are you considering it, though?''

Gavin skirted the issue. Reflecting on the plans he'd made with Pete could hardly be construed as serious consideration. ''I'd be crazy to pass over the opportunity to join Upton's group. Do you know how tough it is to get on their short list, much less be selected?''

''It would be odd if you turned down such a plum position for one in the middle of nowhere,'' John admitted. ''Some might even think a bat had moved into your belfry.''

Gavin managed a tight smile. ''To put it mildly.''

John's gaze seemed to burn a hole in him. ''But you are thinking about it.''

''No.'' But as he said it, he knew he wasn't being honest with John or with himself. ''Only in passing,'' he hedged.

John scooted his chair closer. "Is she pretty?"

"Becky's nice-looking," he countered, preferring to keep his opinion of Aly to himself. "Will it influence *your* decision?"

"Of course not. I make up my own mind. If Becky wants me badly enough, she'll follow. If not, there'll be other women. I'm too young for a wife, a mortgage and two point five kids when I'm just a kid myself. Isn't that right, Lorena?"

Lorena scoffed. "Must you remind me?"

"Besides, no female is going to lead me around by my nose or tell me what to do," John continued.

"Then why do I always have to remind you which drug orders need to be rewritten?" she asked dryly.

"That's different."

Lorena shook her head. "Men," she said in disgust. "Someday, John, you're going to meet a girl who's going to flatten your over-inflated ego. And for the record, I hope I'm around to see it."

He grinned. "Not unless you come to Georgia with me."

"You might be surprised." With that, Lorena went to answer room 515's call bell.

John faced Gavin, his good humor wiped away. "The question is, do you want to go to a town in the middle of nowhere?"

"I don't know. I like to be busy but after running my tail off around here, I'm afraid I'll be bored stiff. I also like solving tough cases, and unfortunately the town's resources are extremely limited. I doubt if they have a CT scanner or MRI capabilities."

He didn't mention how he and Pete had spent hours discussing ways to improve the available medical technology, which had been what had sold him on the idea of going there in the first place. The notion of being in on the ground floor of instituting change had appealed to his pioneering spirit.

"Are you trying to convince me or yourself?"

Gavin gave him a rueful grin. "Both."

"People in small towns need good diagnosticians, too. There are a lot of advantages to recognizing everyone you meet. Just think, your odds of someone stealing your SUV are pretty slim."

Two teenagers had hot-wired his sport utility vehicle last month in the hospital parking lot. Fortunately, he'd been driving on fumes, so the culprits had abandoned his Cherokee ten miles away, but not before they'd managed to damage the transmission.

"There are also a lot of drawbacks," Gavin said. "What would I do in a community where the people are close-knit and know everyone else's business?"

"Fit in? Live a little? Realize there's more to life than medical cases?"

Unfortunately, those were the very things that Gavin feared. He wasn't sure if he *could* fit into Pete's world without his old friend. People would see him and be reminded of the loss of their native son. He had the added disadvantage of not being as personable as Pete. Although Gavin could carry on a conversation with anyone, visiting for the sake of visiting wasn't a skill he'd developed.

Which, of course, brought him back to Aly. After three years, his attraction for her was still strong, but she'd let him down once before and he wasn't about to hand her another opportunity to repeat the experience.

John rose. "Take my advice. Sleep on it."

To Gavin's dismay and disappointment, John's advice didn't help. By the next morning, he hadn't come any closer to a decision than he had the night before. For every reason to accept Aly's invitation, he'd thought of three logical reasons to turn her down.

And yet, for all of his logic, he couldn't shake the nagging sense of obligation that permeated his soul. Only one option would give him peace, but he refused to consider it.

He went about his duties plagued by mental pictures of Aly, Pete and Oliver flashing into his mind at inopportune moments. It was an extremely frustrating morning and became more so when the Reverend Lodge talked of righting past wrongs and getting his affairs in order.

At noon, on Gavin's way toward the cafeteria, John slid into the elevator before the doors closed. "I'm glad I caught you," he said. "I've got news."

Gavin smiled at his friend's excitement. "You're getting married."

"Nope. I just heard about a fellow in family practice who's looking for a position."

Gavin's interest sharpened. "Really? Do you know him?"

"Not personally. It's Skip Donahue."

He groaned. "Not Donahue."

"What's wrong with him?"

"He's referred a few patients over here. I can't believe the man made it through medical school."

John shrugged. "We can't all float to the top. Some sink to the bottom."

"Donahue is definitely in the sediment layer. Whenever I consulted with him about one of his patients, he spent more time asking which nurses would show him a good time."

It didn't take much imagination to picture Donahue trying to steal a kiss from Aly in the supply closet. He didn't like the idea at all, which only proved that he hadn't been totally successful in driving her out of his mind.

John shrugged. "That may be, but even if he passed his exams by one point, he still passed. Anyway, if you find this gal a doctor, then you're off the hook."

"Well, I won't recommend someone like him. He'd be worse than nothing."

"Suit yourself. But remember, if you're working with Upton, why do you care who fills the Hartwell position?"

Why do *you care?* He pondered the question at odd times throughout the rest of the day. It was because of Pete, he decided. Out of respect for his friend and because he shared his high standards, Gavin wouldn't dream of sending someone mediocre to serve the community Pete had loved.

Surely there had to be someone other than Donahue, someone who was a good physician and a decent character. But who?

Surely there was a physician out there who would jump at the opportunity she offered. But how and where would she find them?

Aly climbed out of the hotel pool and dried herself with a towel before wrapping another around her waist. She'd lost count of her laps after fifteen, but she felt just as disheartened as she had before she'd started. Of her three contacts, two had lost interest after she'd explained the situation and the third had spent more time leering at her than paying attention to her story. He'd made her skin crawl and she'd learned not to ignore her intuition. She simply didn't want him.

Then again, she couldn't afford to be choosy. Time was running out.

She dried her hair with another towel and slung it around her neck, wincing at the tug of muscles not used in recent months. If she didn't sleep tonight, she could focus on her aches and pains rather than on what to do about a partner for Uncle Oliver.

As she padded back to her room, she could already hear Izzie's "I told you so". She was going home in the morning with absolutely nothing to show for her three days in the city except a new dress for her friend's wedding, a compact disc and the latest Amanda Quick novel. Only Izzie had known how Aly had hidden her mission to approach Gavin behind a smokescreen of shopping. If things didn't work out, no one would pester her with questions, make sympathetic noises or speculate over the fate of the town's medical facilities.

A young woman with three small children stood in the hallway outside the room across from Aly's. She was clearly having trouble with getting the lock to accept her credit-card-style key and her youngsters weren't helping matters.

"Mommy, I need to go potty bad." A tiny girl, about four, had her legs crossed as she hopped in a circle.

"I know, dear. Just a minute," the harried mother said as she tried the card again.

"Mommy, Mark took my candy," the littlest boy protested in a tone that suggested tears weren't far behind.

"Did not."

"Did, too."

"Did not."

"Stop it, boys," the woman ordered. "I'm going to have to go to the desk and see what's wrong with the key."

"Mommy," the little girl wailed. "I can't wait."

Aly opened her own door with ease and, taking pity on them, offered, "Your daughter can use my bathroom. I'll leave the door open, so you'll know she's OK."

"We'll be fine," the woman said. "Patricia can wait a few more minutes."

Young Patricia shook her head. "No, I can't, Mommy," she wailed. "I'm gonna have a *ax*'dent."

Indecision on Patricia's mother's face gave way to resignation. "All right. Go ahead."

Patricia dashed through Aly's open door. As promised, Aly propped the door open with her suitcase and stood in full view of the small family. If she'd been in similar circumstances, she'd have been wary of the kindness of strangers, too, and she tried to alleviate the mother's worries.

"I had trouble with the door on my first time," Aly commented. "Try pulling the handle up instead of down."

The woman obeyed and the door opened with a quiet click. "Thanks for the tip," she said in obvious relief. "I wasn't looking forward to hauling this group down to the lobby."

"No problem."

"OK, boys, in you go." The two sped off like lightning. Soon high-pitched giggles and the unmistakable sound of little bodies discovering how the mattress could double as a trampoline traveled into the hallway.

"You certainly have your hands full," Aly said.

"Don't I know it."

Patricia reappeared, looking more at ease than when she'd left. "No ax'dents, Mommy."

"I'm proud of you, pumpkin. Now grab your suitcase and go in." She turned to Aly. "Thanks again."

"You're welcome."

Aly closed the door, feeling both envious and sorry for the woman next door. She'd hoped that by this time in her twenty-seven-year life she'd have had a husband and at least one little person to care for, but it hadn't happened. If things didn't change soon, she never would.

A timid knock caught her attention. A moment later, she found Patricia standing in the hallway.

"Hello, there," she told the child. "What can I do for you?"

"Mommy says we should always say thank you and I forgotted to tell you."

Aly found the child's grammar endearing. "You're welcome."

"Bye." Patricia waved her hand and hurried back across the hall. Fortunately, the latch hadn't engaged, so she was able to get inside by herself.

Once again Aly closed the door. Her skin was starting to itch from the chlorine, so she headed for the shower. Before she could get there, another knock rattled her door. This time she found both boys, wearing huge smiles and carrying a handful of jelly beans each.

The oldest held out his hand. "I'm Casey. Want some?"

"No, thank you." Noticing the door to their room was shut, Aly crouched to their eye level. "Does your mom know you're over here?"

They shook their heads. "She's in the little girls' room," Casey informed her. "Does that mean that Mark and I can't use it 'cause we're boys?"

"No, but your mom will be upset when she finds you're both missing."

"But we're not missing," Mark said, his eyes full of innocence. "Mommy said to always tell someone where we're going, and Patty knows we're visiting you." He held out his cupped palm. "Are you sure you don't want any jelly beans?"

"I'm sure. Come on. I'll walk you back across the hall."

Just as Aly rose, their mother barreled out of their room, yelling their names. Catching sight of them, she stopped in her tracks. Using a voice filled with deadly calm, she turned and pointed towards their room. "Get inside this instant."

"We weren't losted," Casey said in an obvious attempt to appease his parent. "You said we should share and we wanted to share our jelly beans."

She didn't lower her arm. "Get. Inside. Now."

This time they didn't argue, but their steps dragged as they headed for their home away from home. It took all of Aly's will-power not to laugh as they stared at her from across the threshold, their lower lips quivering.

"I'm sorry they bothered you," their mother apologized.

"They didn't, but if I were you I'd use my deadbolt lock before they try to make friends with everyone on this floor."

"Believe me, I will."

Aly headed for her bathroom, smiling at the memory of those two sad little faces. Those boys were definitely a handful. Too bad someone hadn't thought of a way to harness such energy—they would be multi-gazillionaires.

She quickly took her shower and rinsed the chlorine from her hair. By nine, she was lounging in her nightgown with her new novel in hand. Before she finished page one, she heard another knock.

She debated answering it, and decided that if one of the children had escaped, she didn't want them pounding on anyone else's door. Without hesitation, she padded across the floor in bare feet, enjoying the feel of the plush pile against her toes.

"Your mom will be angry..." The words died in her throat as she realized her visitor wasn't of the thirty-two-inch variety. Instead, he stood well over six feet.

Gavin's brow furrowed. "I beg your pardon?"

It took her a moment to gather her wits. "Sorry. There're some kids across the hall whose primary purpose in life is to break out of their room." Conscious of her attire, she rubbed the hollow of her throat. "What brings you here?"

"Have you found a doctor yet?"

He certainly didn't beat around the bush. "No," she said slowly. "I haven't."

His gaze was direct. "Then I accept your offer."

CHAPTER THREE

ALY stood in shock, afraid that she hadn't heard correctly. "What did you say?"

"I accept."

Her ears hadn't tricked her, but for some reason Gavin's answer refused to penetrate her brain. In spite of the optimistic attitude she'd shown Izzie, too many disappointments had trained her to keep a tight rein on her hopes. "You do?"

He nodded, his gaze intent. "If you still want me."

"Still want you?" Even if she counted her past hurts against him, he was still a far better choice than the other physicians she'd interviewed. "Of course I do! I mean, *we* do," she corrected herself.

Immediately, her conscience suffered a twinge, but she dismissed it. She'd cleared the first obstacle in her plan and would conquer the next one when it presented itself.

"Please," she continued, her heart pounding with excitement, "won't you come in? We have a lot to discuss."

Gavin hesitated as his gaze traveled her entire length before settling on her face. "We can talk about the details later. If I'd known you were in bed I would have telephoned."

"I wasn't. I mean, I was, but I was just reading. Please, come in." She wasn't dressed for company and unfortunately hadn't packed a robe but, nightgown or not, she intended to cement their agreement before anything caused him to reconsider. In any case, the long white silk garment was far less revealing than the swimsuit she'd worn earlier.

She closed the door behind him and motioned him to one of the chairs by the small table that doubled as a desk.

"We need to talk about starting dates."

"How about yesterday?" She could have hugged him out of relief for solving her immediate problem, but his stiff posture and serious demeanor discouraged her from doing something so rash. He was coming to Hartwell for a business arrangement, not a family reunion, and she would do well to remember that.

To her surprise, his expression softened as a faint smile tugged at his mouth. "I was thinking along the lines of a month."

"A month? I thought you finished next Friday."

"I will, but I can't pack up one day and be gone the next. I have things to do, arrangements to make."

"I understand, but Uncle Oliver is taking a vacation in two weeks. If you arrived beforehand, I wouldn't have to schedule a locum. I'd even drive back to help you pack."

"I can't move out until I have a place in Hartwell," he pointed out. "I thought about contacting a realtor for leads on houses or apartments to rent."

"Don't bother," she quickly answered. Although she hadn't allowed herself to dwell much beyond gaining Gavin's acceptance, she carried the skeleton of her plans at the back of her mind. First of all, she wouldn't go any further with her scheme if word of his arrival leaked out before she arranged the rest of the details, namely discussing this with her uncle. Timing was critical and she intended to methodically set each phase in motion. Some might have accused her of micro-managing but if she wanted to attain her goal of bringing Gavin to town, hers was the best way.

"I've already thought of the perfect solution," she explained. "As you know, Hartwell doesn't have a huge selection of rental property, so I'll arrange for you to have my mother's upstairs apartment. It's quiet, has a separate entrance and at the moment is available.''

He shook his head. ''I don't think it's a good idea. There has to be another option.''

''Not to my knowledge,'' she said honestly. Then again, she hadn't looked. Asking around would have raised questions that she hadn't been prepared to answer. ''If you decide to hunt for another apartment after you've been in town awhile, Mom won't care. This way, though, you can take your time finding a house to suit you.''

''I still need a month,'' he insisted. ''Surely Oliver's practice won't fall apart by then.''

Considering the expense of hiring a locum, it was less than ideal, but a month was better than a year and Gavin was a godsend in comparison to the doctor who'd all but drooled over her during their interview.

''All right. One month. But if you can get away before then…?'' She let her question fade away.

''I'll come as soon as possible.''

Music to her ears. Suddenly, the prospect of a brighter future for her uncle and for her sent her former hurts and anger into the background. She wasn't naïve enough to believe that those emotions wouldn't ever resurface, but at least they were moving ahead.

She stepped closer by two steps to shake his hand and was surprised at the way he stiffened. Obviously, he didn't want her in his personal space, although he hadn't minded it three years ago. Regret poked its icy finger into her chest. If this was the way he wanted it, then so be it. Perhaps with luck and perseverance, she might break through his reserve just as she had when Pete had been alive, but she doubted if they would ever regain the ground they had lost.

What a depressing thought. It was even more depressing when she recalled how she'd once fancied herself half in love with him.

Following his lead, she extended her arm and spoke in the same polite tones she would have used toward any newcomer as she shook his hand. "Thank you enough for reconsidering. I—we—appreciate your decision."

Yet Aly couldn't help but think of how adding Gavin to their practice was an old dream come true. If only Pete were there as well.

"I can tell." His tone was dry as he glanced at their entwined fingers.

She let go and stepped back, realizing she had clutched his hand far longer than socially acceptable. Even with the connection broken, her inner butterflies refused to land. Unsettled by her physical reaction, she rambled on.

"I was going to have to settle for another fellow, so I'm thrilled to have you come to the rescue."

He raised an eyebrow. "Who was the other doctor?"

"A Dr Donahue." She shuddered involuntarily.

"I've heard of him." He cleared his throat. "As for the financial arrangements…"

She hurried to fill in the blanks. "Whatever deal you'd worked out with Pete still stands. You'll have one-third interest in the practice."

"And Oliver is agreeable to this?"

"I have the contract right here." Purposely evading his question, she retrieved a packet from her briefcase. She'd known Gavin would need something more binding than a verbal agreement if they got this far in the negotiation process. Determined to take a page from the Scouts, to be prepared, she'd arranged for her good friend, Jill St James, attorney-at-law, to draw up the proper forms in advance. Fortunately, Jill hadn't asked too many questions.

And yet, as the moment she'd planned for approached, her conscience began to nudge her. The entire affair smacked of manipulation, but being open and completely honest wouldn't help her uncle. He'd been her father figure and, as such, she simply couldn't stand by and watch him work himself into an early grave when the solution hung within her grasp.

If all the cogs slipped into place, her methods wouldn't matter. By the time Gavin arrived, she would have convinced Oliver to accept him and none would be the wiser. If, by chance, someone discovered her machinations, people would be so pleased by the results that no one would mind how she'd stretched the truth.

Aly held out a pen. "Would you like to sign?"

He cautiously took the pages, although his gaze never left her face.

"I assure you, this isn't a trick. No one is going to cheat you. It's all there." She pointed. "In black and white."

He scanned the first page, then the next and the next, until finally he reached the end.

"As you can see, the terms are identical to what Pete offered—one-third interest with an option to purchase up to one half after three years." Fortunately, she'd found the original agreement tucked away in Oliver's files and Jill had used it as a guide to draft a more current document with some slight changes. All it needed was Gavin's name inserted as the new partner and his signature.

"Fair enough. Do you have a pen?"

She handed the cheap fountain pen bearing the hotel logo to him. "Here you go."

Heavens to Betsy! She sounded like a nervous twit. Then again, she had just cause. Everything was falling into place. It was almost too unbelievable.

He placed the papers on the desk and signed the last page. She should have stepped back, she should have moved far enough away to stifle the temptation to trace his jaw line and glide her fingers across his nape, but she didn't. Instead, she clasped her hands together, dug her toes into the carpeting and stared, transfixed, at his wide shoulders.

Perhaps inviting him to Hartwell hadn't been such a good idea after all. She'd thought his rejection had effectively doused her attraction, but she'd been wrong. If she didn't get her weakness under control, she would be in for big trouble.

Too late for second guesses now, she thought as Gavin scribbled his signature on the document's copy. It was over. Finished. Good or bad, she would have to live with the consequences.

"Keep a copy for yourself," she said.

He folded one set of papers and slid them back into the envelope. "Thanks."

A disquieting feeling enveloped her. With their business concluded, their roles had subtly shifted. She was no longer a recruiter out to get his signature on the dotted line. She was a woman with a handsome man in her room, a man who weakened her knees with a single glance.

In that moment, she became acutely aware of her silky, virginal white nightgown and of how her curly hair hung past her shoulders in wild abandon while Gavin wore dark gabardine trousers and a royal blue polo shirt with several buttons undone. He stood tall and exuded power while, in contrast, she felt vulnerable and uncertain. Her memories of standing in his embrace, reveling in his strength and dreaming of the future, didn't help matters. If only he'd switched his cologne to something nauseating or had gained a hundred pounds. Perhaps then she could count her blessings for their separation rather than punish herself with regret.

"Well, then," she said brightly to regain her composure, "this calls for a celebration. I'd offer you a drink, but all I have is orange soda." She quickly filled two glasses with ice and poured the can's contents into each before she handed one to him.

"To a long and prosperous partnership." *And second chances*, she finished as she clinked her glass against his.

"To burying the past," he added.

His comment struck a chord inside her. Was he willing to let bygones be bygones? "What made you change your mind?"

"Isn't it a little late to be asking?"

"No."

"The reasons aren't important."

"Aren't they?"

"Only to me." Gavin drained his cup, leaving only orange-tinted ice cubes behind. "It's late. I should be going. Tomorrow's going to be a busy day."

As much as Aly hated to agree, she did. "I'll see you in a month. If not before."

He stopped near the door. "Do you have my phone number? In case anything changes?"

His doubts were understandable. If she hadn't known how her uncle had rescinded his offer three years ago, she would have taken offense at Gavin's question. "The contract's iron-clad. Nothing will change."

His mouth turned up in the smallest smile. "I was referring to Oliver's health."

Her mind went blank. "His health? Oh, yes. His health." How could she have forgotten? She flashed a brilliant smile at him. "I'll keep you posted in case of an emergency."

"Good." He turned toward the door.

The thought circulating in her brain burst forth unbidden. "I was afraid you might not care what happened to him, but you do, don't you?"

He stiffened. "The only thing I care about is medicine, so leave the psychoanalysis to the experts," he said flatly. "My feelings for Oliver are immaterial. We may work together, but it's going to take a while before I'm comfortable around him. In any case, we just became partners so we need to keep tabs on each other.''

Aly hadn't expected his dispassionate comment. ''Apparently I misread your motives,'' she said, stiffly wondering if she would ever understand his complex character. ''I apologize.''

He took one step closer to her. ''Did you think my signature would instantly make us one big happy practice?''

God help her, but she had. ''Obviously it didn't.''

''You're darned right it didn't.''

What had seemed like the answer to her prayers now took on sinister overtones. What if Gavin's move to Hartwell was only to strike the final blow against her uncle? He claimed that he wasn't out for revenge, but what if he'd lied? Her brothers had always teased her about being gullible. Would this be a case where her flaws would destroy the very person she was trying to save?

She hardened her voice. ''Then why did you agree?''

''Because it's business, Aly. An obligation, if you will.''

Her gaze met his and held it. Surely a man's ulterior motives would show in his eyes, wouldn't they? His steady gray gaze gave her some comfort but, then again, some people had the ability to hide their true emotions behind a straight face. Politicians—and physicians—managed to do so all the time.

''Is it?'' she asked.

''Absolutely. I'm not coming because of Oliver or his poor health. I'm coming because Pete and I had plans and I intend to implement them. I don't like to leave anything unfinished.''

''That's what this is about? Unfinished business and obligations?''

''Yes.''

Aly should have kept quiet, but she couldn't. To her, the

most important unfinished business was the abrupt end of their budding relationship. ''What about us?''

''If you remember, there was no 'us',' he said. ''There was me, and there was you and the Crawford family.''

Although she disagreed, to Gavin it had probably seemed that way. She had tried to straddle the fence and make both sides happy, but in the end she'd failed and had lost something infinitely precious. Now her happiness faded under the glare of his no-nonsense attitude. He was joining her uncle's practice only out of a sense of duty, not because he was interested in second chances.

''What happens when you decide your business *is* finished and that you've paid your debt in full?''

''Are you asking me how long I intend to stay?''

Had she gone to all this trouble for only a few months' reprieve? Had she signed away her legacy for nothing? More importantly, would he leave as abruptly as he had before?

''If we're only a brief stop on your career ladder,'' she said frostily, ''please, let me know now so I can keep looking for your replacement.'' Heaven help her if she had to because she didn't have anything left to use as a bargaining tool.

He seemed amused and she found his attitude irritating. ''If and when I decide I've done all I can,'' he said, ''I'll give you plenty of notice. But don't you think I should move to town before you organize my farewell party?''

''Forgive me for looking down the road further than the next few months,'' she said stiffly. ''We need a long-term solution, not a temporary fix.''

''I agree completely. I simply prefer to keep my options open. For the record, no matter what, I won't leave you in the lurch.''

He made it sound like a promise and she clung to it with both hands. She may have suffered a terrible personal blow, but as long as her uncle got the help he needed she would survive. And if fate smiled on her, Gavin's animosity would fade enough for him to treat her as a colleague and not as an enemy. "I'm counting on it," she said.

"Then I'll see you in a few weeks." As he reached for the knob, the door rattled from the force of a knock. Aly thought of her three half-pint visitors, but this time their mother stood in the hallway with a teary-eyed Mark perched on one hip.

"It's us again," she said ruefully as she glanced from Aly to Gavin. "I'm sorry to bother you this late, but Casey shoved two jelly beans in Mark's nose and I can't get them out. Patricia's asleep and I need to take Mark to the hospital."

Gavin moved in close to tilt the boy's head back. "Jelly beans, huh?"

Mark nodded. He spoke with a distinctly nasal inflection. "Casey done it. He's in trouble, isn't he, Mama?"

"You'd better believe it," she said grimly. She addressed Aly. "I tried to get them out, but they won't budge."

"What about blowing his nose?" Aly asked.

"Nothing happened."

Gavin looked into Mark's nose. "They don't feel like they're too high and I can see them. One's red and one's green. Is that right?"

Mark nodded. "Them's my favorites."

Gavin turned to Aly. "Do you have a pair of tweezers?"

"I think so. Let me look."

Aly disappeared into the bathroom where she'd stowed her cosmetic case and returned holding the silver implement high. "You're in luck."

"Great. Let's see if we can save you folks a trip to the hospital." Gavin motioned the woman and her son into Aly's room.

"Are you sure? I really was just going to ask if you'd keep an eye on Patricia and Casey. By the way, I'm Tonya. Tonya Benson."

"You're not going to believe this," Aly began, "but this is Dr Sinclair and he's *very* good."

Tonya's voice held both awe and relief. "You're a doctor? A real physician?"

"Yes." Gavin glanced at Aly with a raised eyebrow, as if he hadn't expected to hear such an accolade from her. She returned his gaze with a level one of her own, hoping he understood that she meant every word.

After a short but very pregnant silence, he turned to Mark. "All right, sport. I want you to lie down on the bed and hold still for me. Can you do that?"

Mark nodded.

"Tonya," Gavin continued, "sit next to him and hold his hands."

Aly removed the lampshade to allow more light before she knelt by Mark's head, ready to help with whatever was necessary.

Gavin bent over him with the tweezers in hand. "Which color should we get out first?"

Mark's brow furrowed. "Red."

"Red it is. Close your eyes. This won't hurt but you can't move a muscle."

Aly watched him work, noting the steadiness of his grip. In the next second, he held a red jelly bean up to view.

"One down. One to go. Are you doing OK, sport?"

Mark nodded.

Gavin dropped the candy in the nearby trash can. "Here we go again. Get ready."

Mark closed his eyes and once again Gavin worked his magic. "All done," Gavin said once the green jelly bean joined the red one in the trash.

"All done," Mark echoed as he sat upright.

"Are you doing OK?" Gavin asked.

Mark twitched his nose like a rabbit before he nodded. "Fit as a…" He paused. "What is it Grandpa says, Mama?"

"Fit as a fiddle."

"I'm fit as a fiddle," Mark repeated.

Gavin smiled as he ruffled the boy's hair. His actions surprised Aly no end, but the relaxed grin he bestowed on his young patient tugged on her heart.

"His nose will probably be sore for a while," he told Tonya. "But, tough as he is, he'll probably have forgotten about the discomfort by morning."

"I don't know how to thank you," Tonya said, her expression relieved as Mark clung to her hand.

"I'm glad I could help." Gavin crouched down to Mark's height. "As for you, young man, do you know where your elbow is?"

Mark bent his arm to show him.

"Good," Gavin said. "You are not to let your brother put anything smaller than your elbow in your nose or ears or any other part of your body. Got it?"

The youngster's brow drew together as he glanced at his elbow and contemplated his instructions. Finally, his expression cleared. "OK."

Tonya tugged Mark toward the door. "We'd better go so I can get him to bed. Thanks again so very, very much."

"You're welcome," Gavin answered.

"Where are you headed?" Aly asked impulsively.

"Tulsa. As much as I hate to go home," she added ruefully, "it's times like these when I know I made the right decision to move back. You see, my husband left me and, well, you've seen my three. I can use my family's help instead of relying on the kindness of strangers."

"We didn't mind," Aly said.

"Anyway, thanks again. I'll, um…" her face turned pink

"…let you get back to what you were doing before we interrupted. Goodnight."

As soon as mother and son disappeared to their own room, Aly spoke. "I wonder what she thought we were doing?"

"With you wearing a nightgown and the bed turned down, can't you guess?"

Aly's face warmed and she gave an embarrassed chuckle. "I suppose so." And yet she wished they could give Tonya's thoughts more substance. She'd even settle for a kiss, but it would never happen at this point. Gavin didn't trust her completely and, to be perfectly honest, she had her own problems toward him in that area.

"That really was a nice thing for you to do," she said instead. "A lot of other doctors in this situation would have sent him to the ER, but you didn't."

"Don't read anything altruistic into this. I was just trying to save my ER colleagues some work. No big deal."

To Aly, however, his actions, as well as his casual air, were extremely telling. Underneath his façade beat the heart of a caring man whether he wanted to admit it or not.

"When are you going to tell him?"

As Izzie plunked a glass of iced tea in front of her, Aly looked up from the files on her desk. "Soon," she said, grateful for the drink to quench her thirst.

"You said that two weeks ago when you came back from your trip. Oliver needs to know he's going to have company."

"I'll tell him."

"When? Today?"

Aly shook her head. "Today is definitely out."

"Why?"

She rolled away from her desk to pull her scrub-pants

leg above her nurse's shoes and extend her foot. "I'm not wearing my Mighty Mouse socks."

Izzie threw up her hands and raised her face to the ceiling. "Oh, for the love of…"

Aly rolled back to her desk. "Now, remember your blood pressure. I'll tell him, but not today. Between the Carter baby's tummyache, Nate Strong Bear's chest pain and Lucy Morgan's pneumonia, I slept about two hours last night. I can hardly think straight."

"I wish you weren't on call every night."

Aly fought a yawn. "Me, too."

"It's not good for you."

"It's not good for Uncle Oliver either. I'm younger, though, and I can handle sleepless nights better than he can."

Izzie raised an eyebrow, but didn't argue. "He's not going to be happy when he figures out why he never gets paged when he's listed on the schedule."

"He won't if you don't tell him."

Izzie raised her hands in silent supplication. "All these secrets are driving me crazy. I don't remember who's supposed to be told what any more."

"Don't tell anybody anything," Aly advised with a smile, "and you'll be fine."

"Which brings me back to the question of when you're going to spill the beans about our new physician."

"I'll do it *after* Uncle Oliver comes back from his class reunion. I can't mention it beforehand or he won't go."

"Land sakes, girl. You're going to wait until the very last minute, aren't you?"

Aly grinned. "Absolutely. That way, if he does something stupid like have a heart attack or a stroke, I'll have a doctor here to treat him."

"Lord a-mercy, girl. You do like to live dangerously."

"It's called self-preservation," she corrected. "If I break

the news now, Uncle Oliver will have almost ten days to think of a way to ruin everything. I went to too much trouble to let that happen.''

''I don't see how you think you can hide Dr Sinclair when he comes to town. Once he turns off the highway onto Main Street, everyone will know he's the new doctor before his car rolls to the first stoplight.''

''Don't worry. Uncle Oliver will know Gavin is coming well before he actually arrives.''

Izzie narrowed her dark eyes. ''The question is, how *soon* is your definition of 'before'? An hour?''

''I'll give him a few days' notice. Gavin is supposed to contact me with a firm arrival date, and when he does I'll take it from there.'' Aly tapped her pen against her temple. ''Although your suggestion of an hour sounds good, too. I could find out what time Gavin will leave. It takes a little over two hours to get here, provided there isn't any road construction. Now that I think about it, an hour would be the best—''

''Good gravy, girl. Your mama would be ashamed of you for being so inconsiderate. Oliver deserves better treatment from his own niece.''

''I was only teasing,'' Aly admitted. ''To be honest, I'm not looking forward to telling him about his new partner. You wouldn't want to do it for me, would you?''

Izzie held up both hands and shook her head. ''No way, girl. I value my job. He'd fire me on the spot.''

''He wouldn't either.''

Izzie's expression was one of pure skepticism. ''Well, I don't aim to find out. You, on the other hand, are safe. He can't fire you. You're family *and* you're a part-owner of the practice.''

Gavin's contract had whittled her portion to minuscule proportions, but Aly kept the exact details to herself. When she looked at the big picture in terms of her uncle's health and the community's needs, it had seemed a fair trade.

"By the way, how *did* you convince Dr Sinclair to come back? You never said."

Aly avoided Izzie's gaze and spoke nonchalantly. "It was really quite simple. I met with him one afternoon and spelled out my offer. After he'd considered it for a few days, he agreed. End of story."

"If you say so. I'm telling you, though, you may have hired this new doctor, but your uncle is gonna fire him the minute he walks through the door."

"No, he won't."

"What makes you so sure?"

Aly didn't doubt that he would try but, again, Gavin's contract would prevent any such threat from having substance.

"Do you doubt my powers of persuasion?" she countered.

"No, but there isn't any love lost between those two, I'm sure."

"Probably not, but Oliver needs help and he knows I've been searching for another doctor. He's also as eager as I am to fill the position, so he can't blame me for going out on the proverbial limb. Once he realizes that Gavin is our only hope, he'll accept him."

"I hope so."

"The arrangements we made are legally binding. Everyone will come out ahead. No one will lose anything except their stiff-necked pride."

Her situation, on the other hand, was a different story. Although she'd covered her tracks well, the possibility of everything exploding in her face with each passing day was very real. If she managed to hold onto her sanity for the next two weeks, she'd count herself fortunate. Izzie might not know what to divulge and to whom, but her stress didn't come close to what Aly was enduring.

"Have you told your mama?"

"Not yet. I trust Mom to keep a secret, but I don't want to risk any word getting out before I talk to Uncle Oliver. She always liked Gavin, so she'll be delighted to see him again."

Once again, Izzie shook her head. "That may be, girl, but mark my words. I don't care how you sugar-coat your news, Oliver isn't going to swallow it easily."

Aly sighed. "I know." She already could imagine Oliver's anger and hurt feelings. However, if having Gavin nearby added years to her uncle's life, then bearing the brunt of his rage was a small price to pay. "Unfortunately, you and I both know we'd reached the point where we had to do something. This was the best way to handle the situation."

"And where do you propose our new physician is going to park his weary bones after he gets here? Even if we found a suitable place, we can't guarantee it'll be ready for him to move in right away."

"I've got it under control. I told Mom about a friend of mine who wants to come for a few weeks of peace and quiet. Because my place is so small and the phone usually rings off the hook, I asked if he could use her upstairs apartment."

"You told her a *male* friend was coming?" Izzie shook her head. "S'akes alive, girl. Why did you tell her that?"

"Because I was sticking to the truth as much as possible. If she knows her guest is a guy, she won't fill it with flowers or replace the curtains."

"Because she'll be too busy knitting little bootees."

Aly waved Izzie's comment aside. "She won't either."

"Would you like to place a bet?"

Her mother had been dropping a few hints about Aly's

ticking biological clock for the past year, but Aly had point-edly ignored them. Once she'd faced the fact that Gavin had cut off all contact, she hadn't allowed herself to think of romance and family. Work kept her busy and watching over her flighty mother and her stubborn uncle took care of any spare time she'd carved out for herself. Although now she'd have fewer professional demands placed upon her, Gavin had made his feelings toward her perfectly ob-vious. No romance in that direction, she thought.

"If Mom wants to pick out baby clothes, she certainly can. I'm sure one of my brothers will oblige her. Anyway, when I checked on the apartment yesterday, it was spic and span. So, you see, Gavin's accommodations are in order."

"And what about here?" Izzie waved her arms in an all-encompassing motion. "He needs an office to call his own."

"Yes, well, that's proving to be a little more difficult. We need to clean out the empty room at the end of the hallway and—"

"*We?* Do you have a toad in your pocket?"

"I was counting on you to help me, Madame Toad." Aly grinned.

"I suppose I could, but what about the junk you have stored in there?"

"We'll consolidate it with our other supplies."

Izzie didn't appear convinced. "Some of that stuff just needs to be hauled to the dump."

"Then we'll get rid of everything we can't use."

"How? We'll have to borrow one of your brother's trucks and he's going to want to know why."

"I'll tell him I'm on a cleaning binge."

Izzie burst out laughing. "You? Cleaning? He won't be-lieve it."

"Just because I don't like to dust and scrub, it doesn't mean I don't ever clean," Aly protested. "It's tough to be

Harriet Homemaker, especially when I'm rarely at home.''
When her living conditions got too bad, she hired Susan
Gray Wolf, a high-school girl, to capture the dust bunnies.

''And what's your excuse for the mess in here?''

Aly glanced around the room. Between boxes of phar-
maceutical samples, piles of new product circulars and drug
literature, her extra changes of clothes and the large picnic
basket filled to overflowing with the plastic dishes her
mother used to supply them with goodies, her office was a
mess.

''When I move down the hall, I'll sort everything out.
In the meantime...''

''I know, I know.'' Izzie waved her hands. ''Don't touch
anything. You realize that having another doctor around
here will help a lot more people than just Oliver. You, for
one.''

Aly smiled. ''I hope so. I wouldn't mind sleeping until
noon on the occasional weekend.'' What had worried her
most was how easily she'd burn out if she maintained this
pace indefinitely. If that happened, then Uncle Oliver—and
their patients—would be up the proverbial creek without a
paddle.

''Anyway,'' Aly continued, ''I'll tell Morty that we're
cleaning because we have mice and need to find their nest.''

''And he's gonna ask why you just don't call an exter-
minator. After all, you're not too fond of the little fellows.''

Izzie's pessimistic attitude began to grate on Aly's
nerves. Yet, in the receptionist's own interminable way, she
was only trying to help by pointing out the obvious. Aly
couldn't fault her for that. ''OK, so I don't have all the
technicalities figured out. Which is why I need your help.''

''You don't need help, girl. You need a partner in
crime.''

''You already are,'' she reminded her.

Resignation crossed Izzie's face. "If I get fired over this…"

"I'll hire you back. So, will the mice excuse work?"

"Probably, if you let me call your brother. Life would be simpler if you just came out in the open and told Oliver about the new doctor."

The appearance of her uncle in the doorway drove the breath right out of Aly's lungs. "What new doctor?" he asked.

Aly's brain stalled as she tried to marshal her thoughts. She glanced at Izzie, silently pleading for help, but the other woman appeared as nonplussed as Aly felt. For better or worse, her timetable had instantly and irrevocably moved forward.

"Well," she began slowly, "I've found a physician who's willing to move to Hartwell and join our practice."

Oliver Crawford's brown eyes widened in a face where the stress lines resembled a veritable map. After single-handedly managing a busy medical practice for over half of his sixty-five years, he'd earned every crease. "Really? I'd given up hope."

The combination of relief and excitement on his features drained away Aly's tension. Confidence replaced her self-doubt and she slowly began to divulge the details. Once she'd totally sold him on the idea, she'd mention Gavin's name.

But not one minute before.

Oliver sank into a nearby chair, his actions a byproduct of learning to sit whenever the opportunity presented itself because it rarely did. "Where did you find him?"

"In Oklahoma City. He's just completed his residency in internal medicine."

He frowned. "Is he any good?"

"Graduated at the top of his class," she reported

proudly. At least no one could accuse her of settling for second best.

"Then why is he available? I would have thought some other practice would have snapped him up before now."

Aly glanced at Izzie whose eyes flashed with a significant amount of worry.

She purposely assumed an offhanded tone. "Apparently his position fell through at the last minute. It was a case of me being in the right place at the right time."

"When is he coming?"

"In a few weeks. He's going to phone as soon as he has a firm date."

"Single?"

She thought of Gavin's bare fingers. "Yes."

"At least we won't have to worry about a wife convincing him to leave because she's bored here."

"No, we won't."

"I must say, Aly, I never thought you'd pull this off," Oliver said with pride. "This is a shot in the arm for the entire town, and we owe it all to you."

Ordinarily, Aly would have glowed under his praise, but the worst was still to come.

He slapped his knee. "Just wait until I tell Stafford and Dawson. They're not going to believe this. Maybe this talk of closing the hospital will finally die down."

"I hope so, too."

He rose with considerable more bounce than he'd exhibited in a long time. "I'm going to call them right now and brag a little. What did you say this fellow's name was?"

Aly clasped her hands together and glanced at Izzie. Her receptionist's skin seemed to lighten a shade.

"I didn't." She hesitated.

"Well?" he demanded.

Aly swallowed hard as Izzie made a sound that sounded remarkably like a groan. "His name is..."

A shadow fell across the doorway as another familiar body in a dark gray suit appeared in the opening.

Aly blinked to clear her vision, but the man she'd last seen a couple of weeks previously didn't disappear. Shock brought her to her feet and at the same time an impending sense of doom filled her.

Oliver's jaw dropped as he stared at Gavin. "You? What are *you* doing here?"

Gavin glanced at Aly from puzzled eyes, then back at Oliver. "I'm your new physician."

CHAPTER FOUR

OLIVER'S face turned red and every salt-and-pepper-colored hair on his head bristled with obvious fury. "I won't have you in my practice." He turned to Aly. "He can't be the one you hired. Tell me he isn't the one."

Aly braced herself for his wrath. "He is."

"Either send him packing or I will." With that, Oliver stomped to the doorway and stopped to glare up at Gavin. Clearly, he wasn't intimidated by the younger man's towering height. "I'll be in my office. Let me know when he's gone."

With that, he brushed past Gavin with a hearty sniff. A few seconds later, a distant door slammed with the same sharp report as a gunshot.

Aly froze, unable to do anything but reel under the weight of her deed's ramifications. Postponing her little chat with her uncle meant she now had to pay two pipers instead of one, and the man standing a few feet away wasn't any happier than the one who'd left so dramatically. In fact, she'd hazard a guess from Gavin's grim expression that the worst of the storm was still to come.

Izzie broke the silence. "That went well."

Aly stared at the woman who leaned against her cluttered bookcase with her arms folded. "You're joking."

Izzie straightened. "No, really. Oliver didn't throw anything and he didn't have a heart attack. He reacted better than I'd expected."

Aly gaped at her. "I'm glad one of us is happy."

"At the risk of stating the obvious, he didn't know I was coming, did he?"

Gavin's quiet tone didn't fool Aly. She'd worked with enough physicians to recognize the anger lurking under the thin surface of control. She glanced at him and saw the ferocity in his eyes and the stiff set to his shoulders as once again he felt Oliver's wrath and rejection.

Heavens to Betsy. It was as if she'd stepped back in time.

"No," she admitted.

"What kind of stunt are you trying to pull?"

"It wasn't a stunt. I was only trying to—"

"What gives you the right to mess with people's lives?"

"It's not what you think."

"Do you always withhold important information, or am I the only person you leave in the dark?" She tried to answer, but he didn't give her an opportunity. "Is his health as precarious as you suggested, or did you exaggerate that, too?" he demanded.

Izzie broke in. "Oliver isn't in the best shape. I can vouch for that."

Gavin's doubtful expression softened slightly.

"Uncle Oliver's desperate for someone to help him," Aly added. "I'd planned to tell him about you once I knew your exact arrival date. Why didn't you call?"

"I did."

She shook her head. "You couldn't have."

"I left a message on your answering-machine."

"There weren't any messages," she insisted. She'd been too busy to give it more than a cursory glance, but surely she would have noticed a blinking light?

He raised an eyebrow. "It isn't my problem if your equipment is faulty. I did what I said I'd do. I called *and* I came as soon as I could."

"You should have spoken to me in person." Not only was she clutching at straws, she also sounded like a petulant child.

"A lot of good that would have done me," he said in

derision. "When I spoke to you the last time, I got the distinct impression that Oliver wanted me here. Talk about a case of misrepresentation."

"I'm sorry," she said stiffly. "I was only trying to help my uncle."

"By playing God? I don't appreciate being a pawn. If he ever calms down long enough to hear the whole story, neither will he."

"Maybe not, but the point is, we need you," she persisted.

"Correction. You need *a* doctor, not necessarily me, so save your tale for someone who'll believe you."

Izzie broke in. "Children, children, fighting amongst yourselves won't solve a thing. We have to figure out what to do next."

"I'm leaving," Gavin said flatly. "That's what comes next."

Aly drew a deep breath. "No, wait. I'm sorry this happened. It wasn't supposed to turn out like this, but we'll— *I'll*—fix it."

He shook his head. "This entire situation is beyond repair. I should have trusted my instincts. When something is too good to be true, it usually is. Now, if you'll excuse me, I'm going to try and get my other job back."

Aly grabbed his elbow just as he reached the door. Electricity flowed up her arm again and those pesky butterflies began to wiggle inside her. She quickly tamped them down.

"You can't go."

"Watch me."

"We have a contract."

"Sue me."

She stopped in her tracks. She'd never been able to deal with frustration and anger except by crying and tears began to burn her throat like acid. Commanding herself to calm down, she inhaled deeply to regain her composure. "I will."

This time he hesitated. "You can't afford a lawsuit."

She held her ground and raised her chin to meet his gaze. "Probably not. With gazillions lining your bank accounts, I'm sure you can afford to drag this through the courts for years."

He turned back. "Look, neither of us wants the aggravation or the publicity. I'll shred my legal papers and you can destroy yours. We'll both forget this ever happened. Case closed."

She shook her head. "I won't do it."

Gavin's muttered curse referred to stubborn women, but if he thought she would budge from her position, he could think again.

"Why not?" he asked.

"Because we need you," she said, for what seemed the hundredth time. Maybe if she repeated it often enough, he would finally understand. "Once Uncle Oliver cools down, he'll be fine. Just give him time to get used to the idea."

"There aren't enough days in the year or in this century for that to happen. If you haven't realized it by now, you're not as smart as I thought you were."

Desperation filled Aly. Gavin's tone was firm, his mind obviously set in stone. She glanced at Izzie, hoping the receptionist had a magic word or two to sway his opinion. The other woman simply shrugged her slim shoulders.

Aly dropped her hand, hating the idea of her successful plan disintegrating before her eyes. Suddenly, her months of worry, despair and physical exhaustion coalesced into resolve. The events of the past few minutes may have been a replay of the scene from three years ago, but today's drama wouldn't end the same way. Not if she had anything to say about it.

First, however, she had to enlist Gavin's co-operation.

Begging wouldn't get her very far. He claimed not to feel anything for her or her uncle, so she needed to tap into something else. Something important to him…

"Then you're quitting," she said calmly, hoping her strategy would work.

"You can't quit what you haven't started."

"You're here. That's a start."

"A matter of semantics."

"So your word isn't good."

His laugh sounded bitter. "You're a fine one to talk."

She let his accusation pass. "You told me that you were coming because of unfinished business. Am I correct?"

His hesitation was slight. "Yes."

"And didn't you agree not to leave until you completed said unfinished business?"

He frowned as if he saw the direction she was heading and didn't like it. "Yes."

"And didn't you also promise not to leave me in the lurch?"

"Yes," he ground out.

"Which is precisely what you're doing if you walk away." *Like last time*, she finished silently.

A muscle twitched in the side of his cheek. Clearly, he didn't like her reminders and now he fought an internal battle between his wishes and his integrity.

She held her breath as she gambled on the strength of his honor. Softening her voice, she added, "I understand your obligation to Pete. However, Pete's not here, so can't you help his father instead?"

"In case it's not totally obvious to you, I won't be very effective if Oliver doesn't want me. Without his support, my hands are tied."

"He'll support you."

"I don't have your level of confidence."

"I'll talk to him."

He scoffed. "You? Ms Don't-Rock-The-Boat? Miss Polly Peacemaker? Have you ever stood up to anyone in your life?"

She raised her chin. "I just did."

He gave an exasperated snort. "Other than right now, with me."

"You're not the only one who's changed in the last few years. No, I'm not particularly fond of confrontation and I prefer to resolve problems peaceably, but it doesn't mean I'm a pushover. I simply choose my battles."

"So do I, Aly. This is one battle I don't have a snowball's chance in hell of winning."

"Yes, you do."

"I disagree."

Gavin was adamant but, then, so was she. She also had her own ideas on how to handle the situation. "You won't if you don't try," she said firmly. "In any case, this isn't your fight."

"Then whose is it?"

"It's mine. I started this and I intend to straighten it out."

"Oh, really?"

Aly squared her shoulders, irritated by his incredulous tone and disbelieving expression. "Just watch me." She brushed past him to enter the hallway. This time, she had as much to prove to him as she did to herself.

His scent of sandalwood seemed to follow her, but he remained in her office. She glanced back. "Are you coming?"

With a grim face, he followed.

Outside Oliver's door, she paused to draw a breath. Then, without knocking, she turned the knob and walked in to find her uncle staring out the window, his back to her.

"Is he gone?" he demanded.

"No. And he's not leaving." She didn't look behind her,

but she felt Gavin's presence and suspected that Izzie had become Gavin's shadow. Thank goodness they didn't have any patients at the moment, or they would probably have tried to crowd in for the show, too.

"Dammit, Aly. You know how I feel about him."

She stepped closer to his desk. "It's time you faced the facts. You can't handle the practice alone."

"I've done it before and I'll continue as long as necessary."

"The point is, it *isn't* necessary."

A familiar mulish expression appeared on Oliver's face and she continued before he could argue. "I've heard you give advice to other people your age and with your medical conditions. It's always the same. 'Take things easy. You're not a spring chicken any more.' It's time you followed your own recommendations."

"I *am* slowing down. I have you to help," he stated with conviction. "We don't need him."

"We both know that my role in this practice is important, but I can't fill all the gaps."

"Fine. We'll manage until we find someone else."

"No, we can't," she said gently. "We need another physician *now*, not in a year or two. You're tired and worn out and I'm close behind. Without relief, we'll both be useless."

"So we can use another person but, of all people, why him?"

Because he was Pete's friend. Because he was the only one with whom she had any sort of leverage. Because in spite of their history, she still wanted to believe that she could heal the wounds of the past. Unfortunately, she couldn't divulge her reasons without sounding as if she required a long vacation in a rubber room.

"Why not him?" she countered. "Whether you admit it or not, he has ties to this family and this community." And, yes, she'd shamelessly exploited those ties, but it had been for a good cause.

"How could you do this? I don't mind telling you how betrayed I feel. After everything we've gone through together, I never expected you to turn on me like this."

Aly winced under his accusation. In her determination to help her uncle, she hadn't stopped to think about how he would feel. She'd expected him to be upset, but she'd never imagined that he'd regard what was supposed to have been a wonderful gesture as a personal attack. After examining her plan in minute detail, how could she have missed something so crucial?

Yet, she had, and the only place to go was forward. Inhaling a bracing breath, she delivered what she hoped would be the final and crowning argument in Gavin's defense.

"I know you're upset and angry with me, but I've always wanted to do what was best for you, for our practice and for the community." He didn't answer and she pressed on. "Gavin was invited to join Jerome Upton's internal medicine clinic. They wouldn't have offered the position if he wasn't the top pick for the job. Wouldn't you agree?"

Oliver grunted and she took that to mean yes.

"Remember how you fought Forbes when he wanted to drop the hospital bed capacity? And how he fought you when you wanted to upgrade our emergency medical service's defibrillator to a newer model?"

Oliver's nod was brief. She took heart because he was still listening.

"You always told me how your patients deserved the best. You spent countless hours making sure the town had the best equipment. In keeping with your own tradition, I've brought in the best physician anyone could possibly find. You can't afford to send Gavin packing unless you didn't mean what you said."

He pinched the bridge of his nose. "I meant it."

She pressed again. "At great personal and professional cost, Gavin came out of respect for Pete. Can't you accept him for the same reasons?" Oliver didn't answer and she added softly, "Can you do it for me?"

Her uncle turned his sharp-eyed gaze on her. "You're asking an awful lot."

"I know." She actually did. Time was supposed to have helped her uncle accept Pete's death as an accident of his own making. Apparently old opinions died hard.

"You couldn't find anyone else?"

She shook her head. "Not a soul."

The silence was deafening. Aly could hardly stand the suspense as everything hung in the balance of Oliver's decision. It was crucial for Oliver to accept Gavin and she didn't know what she'd do if he refused. She could always move on and let Oliver's practice sink, but she couldn't repay her uncle in such a shoddy manner.

"You've been looking tired lately," he said in a tone as if he were discussing the weather.

Aly was surprised he'd noticed, especially since she'd worked hard to hide her exhaustion. "I've been busy." Busy working…and worrying.

"I'll give Sinclair a try," he said. "But I don't have to like the situation, or him for that matter."

It wasn't a complete victory but it was still a victory. As for Oliver liking Gavin, she was certain the feeling was mutual. Being optimistic, she was equally certain their attitudes would change once they got to know each other.

She hurried to Oliver's side where she planted a kiss against his sunken cheek. "Thank you. You won't regret this."

"I already do."

"No, you don't," she insisted. "Gavin's going to be a

big help and you're going to make sure everyone in the county knows how thrilled you are to have him.''

He met her gaze. ''You're sure about that?''

''Yes, because you're doing it for me. And for Pete.''

''For a trial period only,'' he corrected.

Between Gavin's skills and her working behind the scenes, she was sure Oliver's conditions would soon be forgotten. She could tell him about the contract, but she'd rather wait. No sense in dumping the full load on her uncle at once.

Aly faced the door where Gavin and Izzie stood. Gavin's expression was a combination of surprise and uncertainty, and she smiled broadly.

''I suppose you heard all that,'' Oliver said gruffly.

Gavin nodded. ''Yes, sir.''

''Then you know how I feel.''

''Yes, sir.''

''Were you in on her scheme?''

Gavin stood straight and tall. ''No.''

''I see.'' Oliver paused. ''I imagine you're as happy about this as I am.''

Gavin's gaze briefly met Aly's and his expression was inscrutable. ''The situation isn't what I'd expected.''

Oliver pursed his mouth as he nodded. ''Well, if you're going to work here, be prepared to put in a full day. I won't tolerate a slacker.''

''Yes, sir.''

''And I don't care how good you supposedly are. I'm going to keep my eyes on you. We do things differently around here. This isn't some fancy center where you can order every test under the sun. You're going to have to rely on old-fashioned know-how and not stacks of lab reports.''

Aly opened her mouth to protest, but the slight frown Gavin directed at her forced her to swallow her objection.

"Of course. I'm looking forward to drawing on your years of experience," Gavin said smoothly.

Aly let out the breath she'd been holding. If Gavin had taken offense at her uncle's patronizing treatment, at least he hadn't shown it. Some part of her had wished for the two men to become instant comrades-in-arms, but only a miracle would have made that happen. Still, they were speaking civilly to each other, and for now it would have to be enough.

Once again, the room fell silent. Finally, Oliver cleared his throat. "Don't just stand there, you two. Find the boy a place to hang his shingle."

As a welcome, Oliver's comment left a lot to be desired. However, it served its purpose. Before she could usher Gavin out of the room, Izzie stepped in front of him and extended her hand. "Welcome aboard, Dr Sinclair. If you need anything, anything at all, let me know."

"Thank you," he said solemnly.

As they left Oliver's office, Aly's adrenaline level dropped and the combination of her sleepless night and stressful day caught up with her. With a shaky hand, she rubbed the pit of her stomach and willed her nerves to settle. Thank goodness she didn't have to deal with confrontations like this on a daily basis.

Gavin peered at her. "Are you all right?"

"I'm fine."

"I appreciate what you did in there. It was more than I'd expected."

"Why do you say that?"

He shrugged. "As I said, I always fight my own battles."

"Maybe that's your problem."

He slowed. "I beg your pardon?"

She was still irritated enough to speak honestly, regardless of the consequences. "If you didn't carry this chip on your shoulder about doing everything by yourself, you'd see that lots of people are happy to help you.''

''A chip on my shoulder?'' he echoed.

''You heard what I said,'' she answered. ''It didn't occur to me until now how the great Gavin Sinclair has to do everything for himself and by himself. I hope this incident will finally prove to you how wrong you are. Contrary to what you think, it isn't you against everyone else unless you want it that way.''

''I suppose you think you could have fixed the situation three years ago, too.''

''It may have taken some time, but I was willing to work on it,'' she said tartly. ''You obviously weren't.''

Her barb struck home as he chalked up any reconciliation as a lost cause. Clearly, time had proved him right. Aly may have convinced Oliver to let him stay, but he could predict stormy weather ahead. If not for his debt to Pete, he'd crawl into his SUV and drive until he'd returned to familiar surroundings. Because he couldn't, he would be on his guard and not allow himself to get caught up in Aly's we're-one-big-happy-family fairy-tale.

''I deal with my own actions and fix my own mistakes,'' he told her. ''However well the scene turned out with Oliver a few minutes ago, I can't condone—or forgive—your actions.''

Her spine visibly stiffened under his rebuke. ''I'm sorry you feel that way, but perhaps you've never been in the situation of choosing the lesser of two evils.''

''I have. I just never stooped to manipulation.''

''Bully for you. It must be nice to always make the perfect decision. If you're this angry with us, why did you let Uncle Oliver speak to you as he did?''

''He's just as much a pawn as I am. I'm willing to do my part to make our arrangement work and if that means

I have to bite my tongue on occasion, I will. I hope, though, that dishonesty isn't your normal policy.''

"I wasn't dishonest. I simply didn't explain every little detail. For the record, this wasn't easy on me either. I do have a conscience.''

"I'm glad to hear it. What would you have done if you hadn't talked Oliver into falling in with your scheme?''

"I didn't intend to quit until he did.''

Either she didn't live in the real world, where failure and disappointment appeared as standard obstacles in life's game, or she suffered from an overactive and idealistic Pollyanna complex. "You still should have told me the truth.''

"You wouldn't have listened.''

"You're right. I wouldn't.''

"See?'' She glared at him. "I did what I had to do.''

"So the end justifies the means.''

"In this case, yes.''

He stopped in his tracks. "For the record, I've read my contract. A trial period isn't listed.''

Her face blanched as if she'd hoped he wouldn't have picked up on that small but potentially important point. "I know. Just don't bring it up, will you?''

"Being on probation or the contract itself?''

She pulled him into the privacy of her office. "Both.''

"I get it now,'' he said slowly. "Oliver doesn't have a clue about—''

"Keep your voice down,'' she hissed. "And, no, he doesn't.''

"When were you going to pull this pesky rabbit out of your hat?'' he asked scornfully. "When he tries to fire me?''

"He's not going to fire you.''

"Darned right, he's not. I will say this for you, though.

With all this cloak-and-dagger stuff, you're not making it easy for anyone to trust you.''

"You don't have a sparkling track record in my book either,'' she retorted. "For your information, I only did what I had to do.''

"That's what worries me. Is there anything else I should know about? I presume I have a place to stay.''

As he raised one eyebrow, the fire in Aly's eyes cooled. Clearly, he'd pushed too hard and she'd taken offense at his comments, as well she should. "Your accommodations are ready and waiting, Doctor.''

As she called him by his title, a wall instantly formed between them. He wanted one, he told himself. Aly may have wanted her apology to undo the past, but it wasn't enough. Trust and loyalty were two traits he admired, and at the moment she lacked both. Isolating his professional life from his personal one led to fewer regrets.

Yet, after seeing her as an optimistic one-woman crusader out to save her uncle, her present cool and aloof demeanor made him feel as if he'd disparaged a valuable gift.

Oliver came out of his office and stopped, turning in their direction. "Are you two going to stand here jawing all day or are you going to see patients?''

"I'll be right there,'' Aly said.

"Show Sinclair around while you're at it,'' Oliver told her. "If he's here to work, he might as well start earning his keep.''

"I thought I'd wait until Monday. We need time to find him an office and—''

Oliver waved his hand. "He doesn't need an office until he has paperwork, and he won't have paperwork until he sees patients.''

"Yes, but—'' she began.

"There's no time like the present to start earning his salary. We don't give free rides around here.''

"Letting him wait until Monday isn't giving him a free ride," Aly insisted.

Gavin didn't appreciate being ignored. He hoped this wasn't an indication of how his days would be as Oliver's so-called partner. He wanted to be a valued team member, not someone whose presence was only tolerated.

At the same time, he berated himself for taking Aly's business proposition at face value. Oliver's bitterness had been too great to think he'd set it aside so easily.

He should have phoned the older physician after he'd talked to her the first time, but the combination of guilt and his obligation to Pete had made him swallow her story, hook, line and sinker. Now he had to live with the consequences.

"The best way to swim is to jump right in," Oliver said. "You don't mind, Sinclair, do you?"

"Not at all," Gavin answered.

Aly folded her arms and squared her jaw. "Gavin may not mind but I certainly do. He hasn't even unpacked. All of his personal possessions are parked outside and he's just driven over two hours to get here. Give him a chance to rest and catch his breath."

"Fine. If he needs to rest, let him rest." Oliver seemed pleased, which Gavin considered suspicious. "Maybe we need to hire a doctor who can put in a full day's work. If he has to spend the afternoon *resting*…"

Gavin didn't appreciate the implication. Oliver was apparently trying to stir him into saying something he might regret. "I'm perfectly able—"

Aly drew a breath, as if trying to calm her temper before she interrupted. "You're not being reasonable. No one moves to town and starts their job the same day. Why, he probably hasn't even eaten lunch. You wouldn't start under those conditions, so don't expect Gavin to do it either."

"I'd be delighted to learn the ropes this afternoon,"

Gavin said mildly, surprised to hear her defend him so soon after their argument. Once again, her actions seemed out of character from the girl he remembered.

On the other hand, he wondered if she'd hidden something else from him. Something else that she hoped to rectify before he became aware of it.

"Of course," he tacked on, "it depends on if Aly has time to show me around."

"I don't," she ground out. "But if you want to jump into the middle of things today, who am I to argue? Just don't expect a lot. I thought I had a couple more weeks to prepare."

"I won't hold it against you."

"See that you don't," she snapped.

"Then it's settled," Oliver said. He plainly didn't notice Aly's simmering frustration because he walked away without another word.

"I'll let you start with Izzie. She can explain our office procedures and show you our filing system. If you need me, I'll be around."

"Fine."

While Aly disappeared to call her first patient, he wandered into Izzie's office. The other woman's attitude was much warmer than Aly's had been.

"I heard what Dr Oliver told you about seeing patients today," she said in a conspiratorial whisper. "Don't worry, though. I may find a patient or two for you, but I won't run you ragged."

It was oddly unsettling to have someone, *two* someones if he included Aly, look out for him. He wasn't quite sure what to think or how to react, especially since he didn't know how far their loyalty extended. Regardless, thanks seemed to be in order. "I'd appreciate it."

Over the next hour, he soaked up as much of Izzie's helpful tips and instructions as possible. The receptionist must have also overheard a good portion of his conversation with Aly because she extolled her praises whenever possible.

"Aly's been keeping her eyes open for a nurse to assist you," Izzie said proudly. "She found someone the other day who'll be perfect, but she was waiting to contact her until you arrived.

"And don't worry none about your office. Aly's going to turn her space over to you and have you set up by Monday. Just see if she doesn't. That girl knows how to organize."

Gavin nearly chortled. No one needed to tell him of her ability. It was almost a shame she wasn't in the military. The government could use her talent.

"If you want to go on and get an idea of how you want the room rearranged, feel free," Izzie told him.

He obeyed, feeling strange as he gazed around Aly's cluttered office. The place had a lived-in atmosphere, which was very different from the sterile ambience of the room he'd shared with his fellow residents. The walls were painted a pale blue and a wallpaper border near the ceiling featured Disney characters skipping along a sidewalk. Framed pictures of those same cartoon characters hung in small groupings near her diplomas. The cheery surroundings fit her personality perfectly and he almost hated to redecorate to suit his more subdued taste.

Yet he would need to change the decor at some point. He preferred more businesslike tones, complete with paintings of mountains, streams and other scenes of nature. He wasn't a whimsical-type person, although Aly clearly was.

She strode in, a folder in hand. "Izzie tells me she finished explaining our office procedures."

"So she said."

"Good." She thrust the chart at Gavin. "This lady is asking to see you."

Clearly she hadn't warmed any since he'd seen her last. It was really quite disappointing, although he'd never admit it. "Me?"

She nodded. "Mrs Meadows has been seeing Uncle Oliver, but now she wants a second opinion. Actually, her husband is demanding one. He's with her in the waiting room."

He opened the chart and began scanning the history. "OK."

"I'll put her in Minnie's room."

"Which one is Minnie's?"

"The one with Minnie Mouse on the door."

Something in her voice caught his attention. "Are all the rooms named after Disney characters?"

"Of course. Didn't you notice when you walked down the hall?"

He hadn't paid attention but, then, with all the commotion going on at the time, it was understandable. The idea of facing Mickey, Minnie, Pluto and the rest of the gang nearly made him groan. If he was going to work in a cartoon movie set, he didn't see any point in repainting his office.

"And the adults don't mind?" he asked, thinking of how her design was more appropriate for a pediatric clinic than a family practice.

"Why should they? Most people grew up watching those cartoons."

She was itching for a fight, but he didn't intend to give her one. His main concern was for the patient awaiting him. "Call me when you're ready," he said.

As he reviewed the record, he tensed at the thought of Oliver's reaction when he learned of Gavin taking over one of his cases.

Although the Fourth of July Independence holiday and its associated fireworks were long past, he wondered if the town would appreciate hearing the explosions and seeing the sparks again in August.

CHAPTER FIVE

CONSCIOUS of Aly hovering in the background, Gavin introduced himself to Laura and Rick Meadows. Although he didn't need a nurse to assist him as such, he was operating at a disadvantage. Other than the tongue depressors, cotton-tipped applicators and the otoscope displayed on the counter, he didn't have a clue where to find anything else. Later, he'd go through each room and familiarize himself with their supply layout. Until then, he'd rely on Aly.

According to Laura's chart, she was in her early thirties and had been in poor health for some time. Her slumped shoulders and the exhaustion lines on her face made it appear as if the brief walk had sapped nearly every ounce of her energy.

"We're not unhappy with Dr Crawford," Laura told him, although she directed her comment over Gavin's shoulder at Aly. "It's just that I've been seeing him for over six months now, and I'm as tired as I was when I started. Even if I push myself, I can only handle about half the things I did before."

"So your major symptom is fatigue?"

She nodded. "It doesn't get better no matter how much I rest. I can't shake this constant tired feeling. I'm sick to my stomach half the time and can't eat, but I don't lose any weight."

Gavin paused from jotting down her history. "Any pain?"

"An occasional ache, but nothing more," she replied. "It's more like my muscles and joints are weak."

"We could fill a book with her symptoms," her husband

added. "And sometimes she has trouble swallowing. She doesn't notice it as much as we do, but she's also forgetful, irritable, anxious a lot of the time and depressed."

Gavin scribbled as fast as he could.

"It seems like I have a headache more often than not," Laura added. "And I'm losing more of my hair than ever."

"We came today because she has a sore throat again," her husband said. "She's not running a fever like the kids do when they have a strep infection, but something is causing this. It isn't normal."

Gavin studied the numbers Aly had recorded. "You have a little bit of a temperature. Considering this is a chronic symptom, I want a throat culture." He shot a glance at Aly, who nodded her acknowledgement of his request.

"You're not going to find anything," Rick warned. "Dr Crawford has done several cultures before and the reports always come back negative. He's been telling us this is all in Laura's head, but I don't believe it. She was perfectly fine until about six months ago. Then, almost overnight, she got like this."

"Did anything unusual happen right before your symptoms started?"

Laura shook her head. "Not that I can remember."

He laid the chart down and out of habit reached for the stethoscope around his neck. As his fingers came up empty, he realized his equipment was still stashed in his vehicle. He turned to ask Aly for a spare, but before he could say a word she handed hers to him. "Thanks," he said.

"You're welcome."

The metal earpieces were warm from lying against her neck and her scent clung to the fabric tube she'd used to hide the rubber hose. The overall feeling was as if she'd flung her arms around him, and for an insane second or two he wanted *her* and not an inanimate object draped around his neck.

As if *that* were possible, he thought scornfully. Aly might have her uncle wrapped around her little finger, but if she had to choose between him and her uncle—and she would if they developed a relationship—Gavin would end up with the short end of the stick. He wasn't about to experience that again.

He pushed those images aside to concentrate on his patient's heart and lung sounds before motioning for her to lie down. "I'll poke around for a bit and see what I can find." While he began to palpate Laura's abdomen he said, "You mentioned children. How many do you have?"

"Three," she answered. "Two boys and a girl. Twelve, nine and five."

"Sounds like they're at the age to keep you busy."

"They do, but they help a lot, too."

"Have any of them been ill recently?"

Laura gave a tired smile. "They're disgustingly healthy."

"Have you suffered any unusual family stresses before you started feeling poorly? A death in the family, a job change, financial problems or anything of that nature?"

"None," Laura affirmed.

"Like we've been telling Doc Crawford, the only thing wrong at our house is Laura," her husband said.

Gavin noted no unusual findings, other than he could easily palpate her axillary lymph nodes. He moved away from the table to wash his hands while a number of potential causes ran through his mind. By the time he faced the couple again, his patient had rearranged her clothing and sat up.

"Well?" Rick demanded.

"I'll be honest," Gavin said slowly. "Fatigue is a common symptom for a host of diseases. I'd like to run some tests to rule out as many of those as possible." He flipped through her records to the lab section. "You had a blood count and a thyroid test several months ago."

"The results were OK if I remember correctly."

Gavin noted the figures on the report. None of the numbers indicated a problem. "I'd like to repeat those, as well as perform several other tests that haven't been done."

"Then there's something really wrong with her?" Rick asked, his voice hopeful. "It isn't in her head?"

"I'm not a psychiatrist," Gavin said carefully. "Her symptoms may be a part of clinical depression, but there could just as easily be an organic cause. At this point, it's difficult to make a diagnosis so we'll go through a process of elimination. It may take some time, but we'll sort it out as best we can. If nothing else, we can tell you what it *isn't*, which is sometimes as important as knowing what it *is*."

The look of relief on both Laura's and Rick's faces was humbling, especially when the couple exchanged a glance and Laura's eyes held a suspicious shiny glint. "Thank you." Her voice sounded hoarse. "No one has taken me seriously before."

Gavin met her gaze with a steady one of his own. "I do. All I ask is for you to be patient. The answers won't come overnight."

"As long as I know I'll eventually get them," Laura said, "I can hang on."

"Good." Several possibilities had come to mind and Gavin began to jot down the procedures necessary to either prove or rule out those conditions. "I'll make arrangements for your lab work at the hospital. To start with, I want to check your general health with a chemistry profile as well as repeat your blood count and thyroid tests. I'm also going to order screens for infectious mono and rheumatoid arthritis."

"Mono?" Laura asked. "I never thought of glandular fever."

"One of the primary symptoms is fatigue," Gavin said. "Sore throats are common with it as well."

"You mean, she could be going through all this for a simple case of mono?"

"Yes, but, then again, mono is only one of our potential causes. At least, it's a place to start." He looked up from his list. "Now that you know what I'm requesting, don't panic if the lab tech fills several big tubes."

"I appreciate the warning. I'm not too fond of getting my blood drawn," Laura said ruefully.

He grinned. "Most people aren't. Once I get those results, Izzie will call you to set up a time when we can go over them together and plan our next step."

"Thanks, Doc," Rick said.

"If you'll wait a few minutes, Aly will be back with your lab orders. Otherwise, I'll see you in about a week." Gavin headed for the door, conscious of Aly following.

As soon as the door closed, she spoke. "Izzie's probably explained how she fills out the hospital paperwork based on what you mark on the billing form." He nodded and she continued. "Most of the common tests are listed, but if you want something that isn't, you'll need to write it in the miscellaneous section. A word to the wise, though. Izzie hates illegible handwriting and gets upset if you don't press hard enough for the marks to go through to all the copies."

"She's already warned me." He checked certain boxes and scribbled his preliminary diagnosis before handing the form to her. "I think everything I want for now is listed."

Aly glanced at the page. "A CBC, sed. rate, thyroid studies, chem. panel, mono test, an anti-nuclear antibody and rheumatoid arthritis," she recited, before she tore off the last sheet which served as their record. "Do you know what's wrong with her?"

"It could be any number of things. Epstein-Barr virus, leukemia or lymphoma to name three. We'll have to wait for the lab to give us a direction to go next."

"Then you don't think it's some sort of odd thyroid condition?"

"I'm not ruling anything out, but unless the lab made a mistake three months ago I doubt if her thyroid is the problem."

"I hope you can help her," she said. "Laura was a few years ahead of me in school and was always bubbling with energy. It has to be hard on her to know she can't do a fraction of what she did before."

"I'm sure. In any case, I don't intend to give up. Too many physicians blame psychological origins when they either can't or won't take time to look for a deeper cause."

He was speaking in general, but in light of what had been done for Laura, Aly would probably assume he was referring to her uncle. Her next comment confirmed it.

"It probably seems as if Uncle Oliver doesn't run enough tests to support his diagnoses," she began slowly. "But he's seen a lot during his career and—"

"I'm not finding fault with the way your uncle handled Laura's case. He practices medicine the way he knows how, and I will do the same. Our methods may be different, but I'm sure he wants his patients to get better, just as I do."

"Yes, he does."

"As for Laura, it's time we look beyond the obvious for the root cause. If the positions were reversed, wouldn't you want someone to give you some answers?"

"Absolutely. It's just that I'm a little worried about…" Her voice faded.

She had the most expressive face, he decided. In fact, he'd lay odds that the concern etched on her features was for her uncle and, most likely, his ego.

He finished her sentence. "How your uncle will take the news of Laura coming to me instead of him?"

She avoided his gaze, which meant he'd guessed correctly. "He's not used to—"

"Sharing his toys with the new kid on the block?"

She blushed a becoming shade of pink. "I suppose you could phrase it like that."

"We all have to make adjustments. It happens whenever someone else comes on board." Of course, it went without saying that in this case Oliver's reluctance to accept him made those same adjustments all the more difficult.

"You're right."

He pointed to the form. "Shouldn't you give this to Laura so she can stop at the hospital on her way home?"

"I usually draw the blood myself. It saves them a trip."

"I hadn't thought of it." Between Townsend's clinic and the hospital, there had always been plenty of lab staff available to do the job at a moment's notice. "Sounds like a good idea," he added.

Once again, Aly's skin turned pink. He wondered if she reacted this way to all compliments or just to his. Did she think him so rigid that he couldn't or wouldn't give praise where it was due?

"Thanks," she said. "The patients like not having to wait both here and at the lab. If we have specimens, we call and they'll pick them up twice a day. It's a win-win situation for everyone."

"You don't have to convince me. I'll leave Laura in your capable hands." He turned, then stopped and held out her stethoscope. "Before I forget, I'll give this back."

He wanted to sling the apparatus around her neck and draw her close so that he could kiss her, but indulging his whim would only create more problems. His top priority was to develop a working relationship with Oliver, not engage in a romance with his niece. He carefully, *reluctantly*, draped the object over her open palm, brushing her soft skin with his fingertips. The resultant ache reminded him of what he couldn't have—what Oliver wouldn't *allow* him to have—and he walked away without another word.

Aly went to their small lab where she stored the refrigerated medication and seldom-used equipment. As she located the carryall with her blood-drawing supplies, she wondered if she would ever understand Gavin Sinclair. One minute he was polite and considerate, and the next he made her feel as if she'd said or done the wrong thing.

She couldn't imagine what had caused him to walk away so abruptly. They'd had a polite, albeit cool conversation prior to his return of her stethoscope. A split second later, she'd seen a flash of masculine hunger in his eyes and felt his fingertip caress before his emotions had disappeared behind a mask of impassivity.

A light seemed to switch on inside her, as she finally understood his actions. He *wanted* to say and do things to irritate her because she would then keep her distance. He wasn't as immune to her as he wanted her to believe, and that small but important detail brought a fresh burst of hope to her heart. Now that she recognized and understood his tactics, she wouldn't be so quick to let him be successful.

She returned to Minnie's room with a spring in her step. Both Laura and her husband appeared as animated over their encounter with Gavin as Aly felt with her new-found knowledge.

"He really seems interested in helping me," Laura said as Aly began to draw the necessary tubes of blood.

"He is," Aly assured her.

"You can't imagine how relieved I am. It's like I can see light at the end of my long, dark tunnel," Laura said.

"I'm glad to hear it." Aly mentally crossed her fingers that Gavin would, indeed, find answers for the Meadows.

Then she berated herself for her lack of faith. Gavin was, after all, touted as being one of the best.

"Please don't think we're being disloyal to Dr Crawford or to you, but we had gotten to the point where we had to do *something*, even if it was wrong."

"I understand. Don't worry about it. Getting a second opinion is important, not just for treatment options but also for your peace of mind."

While her uncle normally didn't bat an eye if one of his patients sought out another physician, she didn't quite know how he'd react to Gavin being the other doctor involved. It shouldn't matter but it might, and she needed to be prepared for the fallout if it occurred.

"I for one think Dr Sinclair came in the nick of time," Rick announced. "We were all set to ask for a referral to the Mayo Clinic, but if he can help Laura, I won't mind staying in town. You do think he can help her, don't you?"

Aly knew she'd be asked for her opinion repeatedly over the next few weeks while the townspeople took Gavin's measure. She spoke with confidence without making any promises. "He'll do his very best. And if he can't help, I'm sure he won't hesitate to send you to someone else."

She removed the needle and taped a bandage over the site. "The worst part is over. As soon as I swab your throat, you can go home and enjoy your weekend."

"We will," Laura answered.

A few minutes later, Aly watched the couple leave. She couldn't believe the change that had occurred in Laura in the past twenty minutes. While she still walked with a tired gait, her face didn't hold the same pinched appearance and her despair had lifted. Even her husband carried himself with more confidence.

She went in search for the man responsible for the couple's good spirits and found him poking around the tiny room she intended to turn into her office. "I just sent away two people who are happier now than when they came," she told him.

Gavin looked up from the stack of old medical journals she had piled in one corner. "Are you talking about the Meadows?"

"Who else did you just see?"

He shrugged. "I didn't do anything. Just ordered a few tests."

"Yeah, but you listened and showed an interest. They'd come today to ask for a referral."

"I still may have to give them one," he warned.

"It's possible, but at least you're trying to get to the bottom of her illness."

"Didn't agree with the way your uncle handled Laura's case?" He sounded more curious than critical.

"Not totally," she said slowly, wondering if she was being a traitor by voicing her opinion. "I asked him to run a few more tests, but he does have more experience than I do and she wasn't my patient…"

"So your hands were tied."

"Exactly."

"Well, then, for all of our sakes, let's hope that I discover the problem."

She nodded, then changed the subject. "What are you doing in here?"

"Checking out my future office."

"But this isn't yours. It's mine."

He glanced around the room. "At the moment, I'd say it's nobody's."

"Well, it *is* mine," she insisted. "I just haven't moved in yet."

"It seems a waste of energy for you to move, too."

"Maybe so, but it's cozy in here." At his raised eyebrow, she added, "Don't you know that people have a tendency to fill available space? If I have less to start with, I can't keep as much, and maybe my office won't look quite so disorganized.''

''If I were you, I wouldn't count on it.''

''Hey,'' she protested without rancor. ''There's method to my madness.''

His smile was small, but to her it was a smile nonetheless. ''I'll take your word for it.''

''Good. Now, you'll have to take my word for something else. It's nearly three. Quitting time.''

He glanced at his watch. ''At this hour?''

''Normally we're open until five, but since I was on call last night I'm leaving early. Besides, Oliver is here. If things start hopping, Izzie will page me.''

''I'd rather stay and get ready for Monday.''

''We'll do that after you're settled in at home. You can follow me in your car.''

''I haven't forgotten where your mother lives.''

''Really?'' She shouldn't have been surprised, but she was. ''Then if we get separated, I won't worry about you getting lost.''

''In a town with a handful of stoplights?'' He sounded incredulous. ''Hardly.''

''Actually,'' she began, hoping he wouldn't take offense at her explanation, ''Mom doesn't know you're coming.''

His relaxed stance disappeared and steel replaced his soft, teasing tone. ''She doesn't?''

''It isn't as bad as you think,'' Aly hurried to explain. ''Your apartment is ready and waiting. She just doesn't know *you* are the one who's renting it.''

''Say that again?''

''She's expecting a friend of mine. I didn't tell her your name.''

''All part of your don't-tell-Oliver strategy?''

It was, but it sounded worse coming from him. ''Don't worry,'' she added. ''It will be fine.''

Gavin didn't appear convinced. "Let's get this over with," he said, his tone resigned as if he expected this meeting to be as volatile as the one with Oliver.

Maggie Crawford's two-story Victorian-style home stood on the west edge of town, about a two-minute drive away.

Aly waited for Gavin to join her on the sidewalk so they could walk up together. Although she knew this reunion would go much more smoothly than the one at the clinic, Gavin clearly didn't expect it to be different. He strode beside her without a word as waves of tension swirled around him.

"Trust me," she urged. "There won't be any problems."

Trust me, he thought to himself. Trusting Aly didn't come easy, if at all. Although Maggie Crawford had been a gracious hostess on his first visit, it didn't mean he would see a repeat of her hospitality. If this encounter didn't go well, he would simply move into the run-down motel at the edge of town. As they approached the front porch, he drew a bracing breath.

Aly poked her head inside and called out before she crossed the threshold and motioned for him to do likewise. "Is anybody home?"

"I'm in the kitchen," a female voice answered.

Gavin glanced around the living room. As far as he could tell, nothing had changed in the past three years. The framed photos of family members, including one of Pete, remained on the shelves near the fireplace. A tall glass vase filled with red silk roses rested on the mantel. Thirty-year-old furniture stood in the same arrangement on what had once been plush carpeting.

Aly tugged on his arm. "Come on."

Ill at ease, he followed. He hadn't been this nervous since his first day as an intern when he'd begun his rotation with Dr Alcorn who'd notoriously made his charges' lives miserable. Gavin had always prided himself on being in control, but Aly had wrested it from him with surprising ease. He didn't like the idea, or the feeling it evoked.

Before they got to the kitchen, Aly's mother appeared in the doorway. She wore a flowered cotton dress and a painter's smock liberally splattered with every color imaginable. Her hair remained the same shade of silver and she looked as healthy and energetic as a woman twenty years younger.

"You've brought company," Maggie said as she sent an enquiring smile in Gavin's direction. "What a nice surprise."

"Mom, this is the friend I told you about."

"The one who's staying upstairs?"

Aly nodded.

Maggie came closer. "I'm glad to have you." She squinted as she studied him, and Gavin tensed. "You didn't see my glasses on your way in, did you?"

"They're on top of your head, Mom," Aly answered.

Maggie reached up. "Ah, so they are." She repositioned them on her nose. A second later, she squealed. "Oh, my stars!"

"What's wrong?" Aly asked.

Gavin knew what was wrong—she'd recognized him. The sinking feeling that had become so familiar since he'd driven into Hartwell returned with a vengeance.

Maggie came forward, her steps faltering, her smile wavering. "I don't believe this."

"So much for trusting you," he muttered, for Aly's ears only.

"It will be OK." However, she didn't sound as confident as she had earlier.

"Gavin?" Maggie asked, her eyes wide.

"It's nice to see you again, Mrs Crawford."

"What are you doing in town?"

"He's your new tenant," Aly said. "The friend I told you about."

"That was Gavin? You should have said so, Aly," her mother chided before she addressed him. "I must admit, though, I never expected I'd see you again."

Neither had he. "Your daughter is very persuasive."

Maggie nodded. "She's like a dog with a bone when she wants something. This is one time, though, that I'm glad she's so tenacious."

Her comment caught him by surprise. "Pardon me?"

Without further hesitation, she hugged him. "Welcome back, dear boy," she said. "I've missed you."

Gavin didn't know what to think or say. He patted her shoulder awkwardly as he exchanged a glance with Aly. Her knowing smile and her mouthed "I told you so" finally made everything real.

"It's good to be here," he said simply. And it was. For the first time since his confrontation with Oliver, he felt as if things might turn out differently than he'd suspected.

Maggie broke away. "Did you just get into town?"

"A few hours ago."

"And you're here for a vacation?"

Gavin exchanged another enquiring glance with Aly.

"I recruited him to work with Uncle Oliver," Aly answered.

Maggie's jaw dropped. "You did? How did he take the news? No, don't tell me. I can imagine. Was he awful to you?"

"Aly straightened everything out," he replied. Going into detail seemed pointless.

"I'm glad. Otherwise, I'll have a talk with him."

"That won't be necessary, Mrs Crawford." He was almost getting suspicious of the way the three women he'd met were so eager to smooth things between Oliver and himself. "We just need time to get used to each other."

"You're right." With the subject apparently discussed to her satisfaction, Maggie switched gears. "The upstairs rooms are ready for you. Do you need any help moving in? I can call Morty and Ross..."

"I don't have that much to carry. A few suitcases, a half-dozen boxes and my computer."

"That's all?" Maggie asked. "No sofa, table, chairs, or...?"

He shook his head. "I've always rented my furniture."

"Oh." She paused as she digested the information. "I doubt if Frank at the Furniture Farm rents his stock, but don't worry. We'll find whatever you need.

"And after you're settled in," Maggie continued, without drawing a breath, "I'm going to arrange for a reception. It's the best way to get acquainted." She tapped her forehead. "I wonder if the recreation center will be available next Sunday. I'll call Betty Sue and ask."

"We're not interested in planning a major event," Aly said.

"Which is why you're not going to," Maggie answered sweetly. "All you two have to do is show up at the appointed time. I wonder if I should order white cake or chocolate?"

"Why not both?" Aly suggested.

"Good idea. I'm going to start calling right now." Maggie hurried to the desk telephone. "Have you eaten?"

Gavin's thoughts whirled from trying to keep up with her abrupt changes of topic. "No," he answered slowly.

"I haven't either," Aly added.

Maggie shook her head. "You two should know better. Nutrition is important to good health."

"Yes, Mom," Aly said. "We know."

"Help yourself to whatever is in the refrigerator. While you're in my house, Gavin, I'll expect you to treat my kitchen as your own,'' she finished sternly. ''I won't be responsible for you getting ill.''

''Yes, ma'am.''

''And it's Maggie. Not ma'am.''

''Yes, ma'am. Maggie,'' he corrected dutifully. He hadn't realized how one petite sixty-something-year-old lady could make him feel as if he'd committed an unpardonable sin by missing a meal. Even Lorena hadn't turned a forgotten lunch into a major crime.

Maggie wagged her schoolteacher finger. ''Dinner is at seven and I'll expect you both to be here on the dot.''

''Dinner?'' he asked. He'd expected to forage for himself.

''Seven o'clock,'' Aly repeated.

''And don't forget our Sunday brunch.'' A clock chimed in the background and Maggie threw up her hands. ''I do wish you'd given me more notice about Gavin. There's more to a welcoming party than meets the eye.'' Without giving either of them a chance to respond, she scurried from the room, presumably in search of a phone.

Aly gave him an apologetic shrug. ''As a note of warning, my mother operates on impulse and generates all sorts of plans, but she doesn't always follow through. She has a tendency to get sidetracked.''

''Unlike her daughter, I presume?''

Aly grinned. ''I guess you could say so.''

''Then there's a good chance there won't be a reception?'' He hated the idea of being on display.

''It may be rather unorthodox, but Mom will arrange a reception in your honor,'' she assured him. ''You're part of the community now, so you'd better get used to the idea.''

But would he?

CHAPTER SIX

"YOU look worn out, dear."

Aly smiled at her mother's well-meant comment as she helped her clear away the leftovers from Sunday's regularly scheduled family brunch. This week, however, had brought a few changes. Gavin had joined their circle, but the head of the Crawford clan was noticeably absent. If Maggie hadn't mentioned in an aside that Oliver had telephoned his regrets because he was too busy packing to leave town for his class reunion, Aly would have worried about him. As it was, the reasons for his non-appearance were feeble at best. Her uncle would get a piece of her mind the next time she saw him.

"I am tired," she admitted. "The last few days have been terribly busy. Between reorganizing the office and being on call, I can hardly keep my eyes open."

After helping Gavin empty his car on Friday evening, she'd been running at full steam. Reorganizing the clinic, seeing patients at the hospital and checking on Oliver had filled her days and most of her nights. She'd lived on three hours of sleep since before Gavin had arrived, and at the moment she wanted a nap more than anything.

Well, maybe not more than *anything*, she amended as Gavin walked into her line of vision and sat on the lawn chair in front of the glass door. If she had to choose between Gavin treating her like the woman of his dreams or taking a nap, those few hours of shut-eye would fall to second place.

"Don't wait too long before you let Gavin do his job," Maggie scolded.

"With Oliver gone next week, I won't." Aly stood at the table and stared outside at the rest of her family, relaxing on the patio. Her brother Morty sat with his new wife, Georgia, her other brother Ross and his wife Hope in a loose circle. Yet, in the midst of their easy banter, Gavin didn't join in the conversation. Instead, he stared at Ross's children playing in the nearby sandbox. Rufus, their gentle cocker spaniel, lay on the grass a few feet away as he, too, watched over his charges.

Maggie joined her at the table. "Gavin is still as quiet as ever, I see."

Aly nodded. "I'm sure he's uncomfortable because Uncle Oliver made a point of not coming."

"Your uncle is having a hard time right now," Maggie told her gently. "He's torn in several different directions now that Gavin is back in the picture."

"I know." She sighed. "Everything seemed so simple when I planned this. Uncle Oliver needed help and because Gavin had liked us well enough at one time, he was the perfect doctor to recruit."

"He was," Maggie agreed. "If the men didn't have a history of their own to deal with."

"But that's just it, Mom. They shouldn't *have* a history. Gavin wasn't responsible for Pete's death."

"We both know that, but your uncle has this irrational idea that Gavin should have saved him. Until he gets past that, he'll always bear a grudge."

"And make Gavin's life miserable in the meantime," Aly said glumly. "Maybe I shouldn't have brought Gavin here. I've basically ruined his life."

Her mother's eyes twinkled. "I doubt if it's totally ruined or if it's *pure* misery. After all, he has you around to brighten his days."

Aly smiled as she trained her gaze on Gavin. "I'm not

sure I can do the job. He closes himself off from people. He's strictly a business sort.''

''People who've been hurt have a tendency to do that. You just have to decide if he's special enough to save.''

Aly recognized the signs of her mother's fishing expedition. Gavin was by far the most special man she'd ever known, but she wasn't going to admit it to anyone, especially not her mother.

''That's just it,'' she blurted out. ''I want to be angry at him for what happened before and some days I am, but then he'll turn around and do something sweet and considerate and I'll forgive and forget. Sometimes I think my grip on reality is slipping.''

Maggie laughed. ''No, dear, it's not. I understand why you'd be upset with him, but you're too soft-hearted to hold a grudge. You simply have a forgiving nature. Accept it as part of who you are.''

''I guess,'' Aly said glumly, wishing it was otherwise.

''Do you know what his name means?''

Used to her mother's bent for twists and turns in her conversations, Aly followed along. ''No.''

''According to one baby book, Gavin means white hawk. Do you remember when Mr Gilchrist retired from the Fish and Game Service with the hawk he'd rescued?''

''A little.''

''Gavin reminds me of that hawk.''

''Really? How?''

Maggie steepled her hands and tapped her mouth. ''If I remember my facts, Mr Gilchrist had to have all sorts of government permits to keep the creature. The species is protected by state and federal law, you know.''

Aly sighed, wishing her mother didn't have a tendency to drift along tangents.

''Anyway, they build their nests in the crotch of a tree and they rarely use the same nest site. The goshawk, in particular, has been reported to attack humans who approach their nests. Mr Gilchrist also told our ladies' group that hawks are very excitable in captivity, although the young birds can become quite tame.''

''Your point being?'' Aly asked.

''It's obvious, dear. Gavin has a tendency to leave everything he has behind. He left Hartwell three years ago without a backward glance, and when he returned he did the same. To round out the picture, he even *rents* his furniture.''

''Lots of people do that in the city,'' Aly defended. Although she didn't know specifically of any, it had to be a fairly common practice or stores wouldn't offer the program.

''I'd also bet that you two have exchanged words a time or two,'' Maggie said slyly. ''Maybe when you said something that struck a little close to home?''

Her comment was uncannily accurate. He always objected whenever she probed his feelings. ''I suppose you're going to tell me he's excitable in captivity.''

''I'm only suggesting it. Aren't you seeing signs that he's having a hard time adjusting? A difficult time settling in? And, I dare say, he's not particularly trusting at the moment.'' She motioned outside. ''Mr Gilchrist's hawk was the same way.''

''Well, yes, but—''

''But there's hope,'' Maggie said confidently. ''Hawks can be tamed and I'm counting on my daughter to help the one outside settle into his new surroundings.''

Aly rolled her eyes. ''Heavens to Betsy, Mom. I don't know the first thing about taming hawks.''

''It doesn't matter. Everything and everyone responds to kindness and love.''

''What makes you think I can change him if he doesn't want to be changed?''

Maggie stared outside. "Ah, but I think he does."

Aly followed the path of her mother's gaze. For a moment she thought she saw longing on Gavin's face as he watched the children. He'd hung on the outskirts when Pete had first brought him to Hartwell, but she'd brought him around. Could she do it again?

"When I think of how his parents shuttled him from one nanny to another, from one boarding school to another, I just want to...to slap them both silly," Maggie finished vehemently.

Aly did, too. The thought of a young boy being treated in such a manner sent chills down her spine. As far as she was concerned, slapping was nowhere near enough punishment for the two adults who were supposed to have cherished him and been his champions. Her children, when and if she ever had any, would know a mother's love.

"Besides, dear, I have faith in you."

Her mother's confidence wasn't inspiring. She'd already disappointed Uncle Oliver by her secretive actions. All she needed was to disappoint another person in her life. "Oh, Mom."

"Don't 'oh, Mom' me. I know what I'm talking about. You've always faced adversity without backing down. Of course, there were those times when you went against my better judgement—"

"Like now?"

Maggie hugged her daughter. "You do like to go where angels fear to tread, but it's time to right wrongs and let dear Pete rest in peace. He would be furious if he knew we'd allowed the situation to slide this long. He thought the world of Gavin."

Aly remembered. Surely a supernatural force was at work for her to have cooked up this idea in the first place.

"Now, go on outside and keep Gavin company."

She bussed her mother's cheek before she slid open the

glass door and stepped outside. Gavin raised his head at the noise and his gaze held traces of relief. She plunked into the lawn chair beside him and tried to think of a way to politely extricate Gavin from her family circle. Although she loved them dearly, Gavin would fare better if she limited his exposure to small doses.

''I'd offer to show you the local sights, but you'd have to drive,'' she said.

Morty chuckled. ''She's telling the truth, Gav. Get Aly in a car and if she's not behind the wheel she'll be fast asleep within fifteen minutes.''

''I'm not that bad,'' she protested.

''Close,'' Ross added.

She ignored her brothers' teasing. ''How about a walk instead?''

Gavin sat up straight. ''Sounds great. Where to?''

She hadn't expected him to agree so readily and she almost wished she could rescind her offer. Although rescuing Gavin seemed far more important than her exhaustion, it didn't stop her from savoring the few moments of being off her feet.

''We'll go around the block.'' She addressed her family as she rose. ''See you guys shortly.''

Amid a chorus of goodbyes and grubby kisses from her oldest niece, four-year-old Gretchen, Aly and Gavin rounded the corner of the house and set off down the front sidewalk.

''I hope your mother doesn't feel like she has to cater to me,'' he said.

''She doesn't. For all her talk about good nutrition, the family brunch on Sundays is the only time I don't worry about her eating. She tends to become so immersed in her projects that she forgets about meals, although she's always whipping together some sort of dessert. Be prepared to see lots of cookies and the like at the clinic. Some are sugar-free and some aren't.''

''What about your uncle?''

''He's a different story,'' she said wryly. ''He eats at the diner a lot and doesn't pay as close attention to his diet as he should. We scold him, but…'' She shrugged.

''He does what he wants to,'' he finished.

She grinned. ''Stubborn is his middle name.''

''I noticed,'' he said wryly.

As they ambled down the sleepy, tree-lined street, Aly was reminded of the differences between Hartwell and Oklahoma City. ''Have you missed the hustle and bustle yet?'' she asked.

''I have,'' he answered. ''My apartment was a few blocks from the hospital and I heard every ambulance siren. After a while it became comforting background noise.''

Sirens, police or ambulance, were a noteworthy event in Hartwell. ''And you don't have it here.''

''No, I don't. I turned the radio on but the local station goes off the air at midnight.''

She giggled at his mournful note. ''So much for life in the fast lane.''

He smiled. ''Yeah.''

As they neared a two-story frame home not far from the corner, loud voices broke the peaceful atmosphere. Guessing at the cause, Aly sighed and motioned in the direction of the commotion.

''If you think Oliver is stubborn, you're about to meet two people who wouldn't know compromise if it bit them on their behinds.''

The nearest house boasted plain white clapboard siding and an authentic Indian teepee in the front yard. The structure to its right was identical in size and shape, although it was painted yellow and had a profusion of flowers lining the foundation. An elderly man and woman argued over a hedge of lilac bushes separating their respective properties. She brandished a cane and he wielded a chain-saw.

Gavin laid a hand on Aly's shoulder. "Are you sure you want to get in the middle of this?"

"They're harmless."

"From the way she's swinging her stick and he's pointing that saw, I don't think I'd agree," he said wryly.

"They just need someone to mediate. It happens all the time between those two." Aly walked into the fray. "What's going on, Miss Peabody? Mr Gray Horse?"

Hedda Peabody was a quintessential retired librarian. She wore sensible shoes, a dark dress with a lace collar and a cameo at her throat, regardless of time or place. She fashioned her gray hair in a bun on the top of her head.

"This man," she declared, pointing at Joshua Gray Horse, "is killing my lilac bushes."

"Better the bushes than me," Joshua growled. He only stood a few inches taller than Hedda, but he carried himself with all the regal bearing of his Native American ancestors. His thinning gray hair hung past his shoulders and a beaded band circled his head. He wore blue jeans and a bright Aztec-print cowboy shirt, and sported a red bandanna around his neck.

Hedda raised her chin. "My bushes are not killing you. It's all that smoking of your so-called peace pipe and those weeds you burn in your house."

"My herbs are not weeds. If you actually read any of those books in the library, you'd know that."

"Hah! I'll have you know—"

Aly moved in close and raised her hands. "Please. What's the problem this time?"

Joshua pointed to the lilac bushes. "Her flowering things pollute the air outside my window. I can't catch my breath because they stink."

"Then close your window," Hedda retorted.

"If the Great Spirit wanted us to live in airless houses, he wouldn't have invented glass panes to slide up and down."

Hedda raised her own age-spotted hand and pointed. "See what he's going to do? He wants to use his chainsaw and turn my beautiful bushes into twigs."

"I'm trimming them," he said. "They'll grow into my house if I don't."

"Don't be ridiculous," she snapped. "You intend to mutilate them so they'll die and you'll finally get what you want. For my babies to be gone."

"I have great respect for Mother Earth's bounty, even the things that smell bad." He glared at Hedda.

Aly studied the bushes. As Joshua had claimed, several of the branches brushed against the side of his house. Plants and shrubs weren't her specialty, but even she could see that if something wasn't done, by next summer, they would completely block out his window.

"Aren't you supposed to trim the bushes quite vigorously in order to stimulate growth?" she asked.

"In the early spring," Hedda sniffed. "Not at this time of year. If my bushes die, I will hold you responsible. For your information, they are irreplaceable. They're cuttings from the Peabody family home in North Carolina."

Joshua straightened to his full height. "I still say it's better if the bushes die and not me."

"You're not going to die, you old codger. If you don't have any trouble breathing around horses then you can handle my lilacs just fine."

Gavin spoke. "That's not necessarily so, Miss Peabody." At their enquiring glances, he introduced himself. "Speaking as a physician, Mr Gray Horse could easily be allergic to lilacs and not horses."

Hedda sniffed. "I might have known you men would stick together."

"No," Aly protested. "Dr Sinclair is right."

"Well, then, Joshua can simply keep his windows closed."

Joshua bristled. "Are you telling me that I can't walk in my own yard either? Maybe you'd rather I tether my horse to nibble down the grass since I can't come out to use the lawnmower. Or, better yet, I'll get a goat. They love flowers and yours look especially tasty."

"Don't you dare bring a goat here," Hedda warned.

"Please," Aly interrupted. "Let's be reasonable."

"I'm trying, but she won't listen to reason." Joshua spoke with disdain. He turned toward the nearby porch step, stumbling a little on the way.

Aly faced Hedda. "If Mr Gray Horse is having health problems, you wouldn't want to be the cause of them, would you?"

Hedda pursed her mouth as if she couldn't decide. "I suppose not. But I can't lose my bushes. They're a part of my family." Her chin quivered and her voice wobbled.

Aly glanced at Joshua, but he leaned against the pillar with his eyes closed.

"Why don't you move them to another location?" Gavin suggested.

"I was going to say the same thing!" Aly exclaimed, smiling at Gavin for speaking her thought aloud. "You could replant them on the other side of your yard where Mr Gray Horse wouldn't have them under his nose."

Hedda folded her arms. "I lived here first. I shouldn't have to tear out my shrubs because *he* doesn't like them."

"If it will keep peace between you," Aly began, "wouldn't it be worth it?"

"Nothing is worth losing my heritage," Hedda said loftily.

"Fine. Let her keep her blasted stink plants," Joshua

said from his corner. "Just send the bill for my funeral expenses to her." With that, he toppled over onto the porch.

With Hedda's "oh-mi-gosh" echoing in Aly's ears, she dashed toward Joshua, but Gavin reached him first. He immediately began unbuttoning the man's shirt. "Can you talk?" he asked.

"Yes," Joshua drew out.

"What's wrong?"

"Sick to…my stomach. Weak."

Aly could see the sheen of perspiration on his face and the tremor in his extremities.

"Any history of heart problems?" Gavin asked him.

As Joshua shook his head, Aly supplied her own facts. "He's a diabetic. It could be an insulin reaction."

"Does he test his blood?"

Joshua licked his lips. "In the house."

"I'll be right back." Aly ran inside, glancing through each room as she made her way through the house. She guessed he would keep his testing equipment in either the bathroom or the kitchen, and she patted herself on the back when she found the kit on the table. She riffled through the box's contents, pleased to see a small vial of glucose tablets for emergencies such as this.

Kneeling beside him once again, she slipped a tablet into his mouth while Gavin pricked Joshua's finger with a practiced motion. "It's thirty," he reported a minute later. "Definitely hypoglycemic."

Joshua's shakiness began to subside and he wiped his upper lip. "That hasn't happened for a long time," he said.

Hedda wrung her hands as she hovered over them. "Is he going to be all right?"

Gavin sat back on his heels to study his patient. "He'll be fine. Did you take too much insulin?"

Joshua sat up with Aly's help and leaned against the porch's pillar. "The usual amount. But I didn't eat when I should have. I had opened my window and saw the branches scraping against the side of my house. I was going to trim just a few so they wouldn't scratch off the paint, but she came out of her house and started screaming like a banshee.''

"And you couldn't walk away," Aly guessed.

Joshua shook his head. "My honor was at stake."

"I wasn't screaming," Hedda said primly. "I was merely trying to get your attention."

"Well, you did." Joshua closed his eyes.

"Are you sure he's all right?" Hedda sounded worried. "I had no idea he was a diabetic. But I do recall reading something about how Native Americans are nearly three times more likely to develop the disease than other Americans."

"Your statistics are right," Aly said. "But Mr Gray Horse will be fine. He just needs to eat."

"Well, then, I suggest you let the man enjoy his lunch," Hedda said, before she approached the step and patted Joshua's hand. "Don't worry about a thing. I'll call the nursery first thing in the morning to move my shrubs. Perhaps if you're feeling better later, you might come over so we can choose a spot where my lilacs won't bother you."

Joshua blinked in stunned surprise. "I appreciate it."

"Not at all. We can't have you getting upset and aggravating your condition." With that, Hedda straightened. "Goodbye for now."

As soon as she'd marched into her house, Aly glanced at Joshua, who was clearly as flummoxed by his neighbor's change in attitude as she was.

Gavin chuckled. "I think your troubles are over, Mr Gray Horse."

"Something's changed," he answered, clearly bewildered. "Do you think she believes that our argument brought on my drop in blood sugar?"

"Apparently so," Gavin replied. "Don't worry, though. I won't tell her differently."

Joshua's smile became broad as if he'd finally realized the ramifications of Hedda's change in attitude. "I would be forever in your debt."

Aly insisted on staying a few more minutes until she was certain that Joshua wouldn't suffer any other lasting effects. After watching him drink a glass of orange juice, she said goodbye and encouraged him to see one of them next morning if he had any more problems.

"So much for a quiet walk," Gavin said as they headed back toward her mother's house.

"No kidding. They're usually not as exciting, although ER duty on a Saturday night can get interesting."

"Speaking of the ER, tell me about the local hospital."

"It hasn't changed since you were here. They've upgraded a few pieces of equipment, but not much else. Without doctors moving into town, it's a struggle to stay afloat."

"What about the lab and Radiology?"

"The lab does the basics on site and refers the rest to another facility. Our two X-ray technicians take films and send them to the radiologist at Guymon to be read. We're on a bimonthly circuit for a mammography unit but we don't have any CT scan or MRI capabilities."

"Not even portable units?"

She shook her head. "We don't have the demand. If someone needs those tests, they're usually ill enough to require more medical services than our facility can provide. It's more cost-effective to send the patient to Guymon."

"I see. Would those departments be interested in adding more procedures?"

"I'm sure they would. Loni is the X-ray supervisor and

Tom is in charge of the lab. Both have always been very accommodating, but you won't know until you ask.''

"I will."

As they approached the house, she yawned. "Excuse me. I didn't mean to do that."

"Bored with the company?"

"Never," she said vehemently, recognizing sincerity underneath his teasing tone. "The past few days have been busy."

"Are you on call tonight?" he asked.

"No, but…" After a brief pause, she finished. "You'll find out soon enough anyway, so I might as well tell you."

"Tell me what?"

"My uncle is on the on-call schedule, but I have this arrangement with the hospital. You see—"

"They call you instead."

She stared at him. "How did you guess?"

"You're tired, drink more caffeine than anyone I know, and when I asked Izzie point blank, she told me."

"She wasn't supposed to say a word."

"I'm a partner, remember? That means I'm supposed to know what's going on."

Duly chastised, she stared straight ahead. "I've been trying to shield my uncle from so much that I guess it's become habit."

"Habits are made to be broken."

"Yes, well, my uncle would be devastated if he thought he wasn't pulling his own weight."

"But he's not."

"It doesn't matter," she insisted.

"Yes, it does. You're not very effective if you're burning the candle at both ends."

She gritted her teeth. "This is the way I want it, so don't you dare lecture me."

"I won't, but this situation is going to change."

Aly halted in her tracks and grabbed his arm to keep him from marching on. "If you tell Uncle Oliver what I've been doing, he'll be crushed."

"Why are you so intent on protecting him?"

"Because he's been like my father for as long as I can remember," she said simply. "My dad died when I was two and a year later Oliver's wife, Charlene, passed away. Although we lived separately, my uncle did father things with me just like my mother did mom things with Pete. He looked after us and now it's my turn to repay him.

"You haven't seen the change that I have over the past few years," she added. "He's already unhappy about his physical limitations. I don't want to want to make him feel more inadequate."

Pinning her under his gaze, he hesitated. Aly waited for his verdict. If Gavin didn't support her in this, she didn't know what she'd do.

"If it means that much to you," he said slowly, "I won't divulge your secret."

She closed her eyes and let out her breath. "Thank you."

"But we'll work out a system tomorrow," he told her. "First thing in the morning."

"It's a deal."

"And you'll hand over your pager right now."

He extended his hand, palm up, and she stared at it as if it were a snake. "Now?"

"Now," he said firmly.

"But what if—?"

"If I can't handle a situation, I'll call you."

Still she hesitated. The small box clipped to her waistband suddenly weighed ten pounds instead of a few ounces. The burden of responsibility was heavy, she decided, but to give it up? On such short notice?

Yet the prospect of an evening of uninterrupted sleep—sixteen hours if she hurried home and hopped into bed immediately—was as tantalizing as a thick, gooey, hot fudge sundae to a person on a strict diet. It didn't take any effort to imagine herself resting on her soft mattress, entangled in a cocoon of soft cotton sheets.

The only way to improve upon her picture was if Gavin lay beside her.

She touched the pager. "Do you promise?"

He held up his other hand as if swearing an oath. "I do." He waggled his fingers. "Come on. You know you want this."

She did. Absolutely, positively. Telling herself to act before she talked herself out of accepting his offer, she unclipped the unit and dropped it in his palm. "Mrs Durley has a tendency to eat too much on the weekends. She comes into ER with heartburn and swears it's a heart attack. You'll have to—"

"Order the usual tests, and if they're negative, I'll prescribe antacids and send her on her way."

"And if Donald Merriweather comes in—"

"I'll deal with the problem. Whatever it is." Because they had reached their starting point, he guided her toward her car parked alone on the street.

"Looks like Morty and Ross went home," she said.

"Which is exactly where you're going." He opened the driver's door. After she slid in, he closed it. "I'll see you in the morning."

"If not before," she corrected.

"If not before," he repeated. "Sweet dreams."

Aly reached for the key, then stopped as she realized how they had talked as easily as they had so long ago. Maybe Gavin was beginning to see how life would be more enjoyable if he allowed people close to him. Suddenly, an impulsive idea began to take shape. "Wait a minute."

He leaned closer so that his face hovered near the open window. "What now?"

She stretched and planted a soft, lingering kiss on his cheek. His skin was slightly rough and he smelled of sandalwood and the great outdoors. He jerked his head so that her mouth landed on the edge of his before she settled back in her seat. "Thanks," she said softly.

"You're...you're welcome."

She'd hoped her kiss would knock a chunk off his reserve, and from his stunned expression she'd been successful. Now all she had to do was think of an encore.

CHAPTER SEVEN

THREE weeks later, Aly was waiting in her office for Oliver to arrive. Several issues had arisen during the past ten days that required attention, and unfortunately catching Oliver had become a near-impossible feat.

She hadn't realized how easy it had been to make major decisions affecting the practice when he came early and stayed late, even though it wasn't necessary for him to keep those long hours. He'd stop by her desk and they'd talk about patients, protocol, interesting medical updates and life in general. Gavin's presence had changed their routine and not for the better.

Oliver now chose to arrive moments before his first appointment and left on the heels of his last. She'd teased him about his "banker's hours of nine to three" and he'd responded with, "You wanted me to slow down and take things easy, so don't complain because I am."

He'd needed time to adjust and she'd been willing to give it to him. Everyone had. However, enough was enough. She couldn't let her concerns slide any longer.

"He's coming," Izzie hissed as she stared through Aly's window overlooking the parking lot.

Aly rose. "Wish me luck."

Izzie gave her a thumbs-up sign and a whispered "Go, girl" as the back door slammed. Hearing Oliver's measured pace, Aly moved to the doorway of her office, ready to intercept him. To her surprise, his skin color was pasty and he limped heavily.

"Where's Sinclair?" he demanded.

Her rehearsed opening flew out the window, but she refused to be daunted by his grumpy mood. Today things around here would change or her name wasn't Alison Margaret Crawford.

"I'm sure he's on his way. Why are you limping?"

"I have a sore toe. Why isn't he here? It's almost nine."

"He's meeting with the lab and X-ray techs at the hospital. He wants to see if they can—"

Oliver waved his hands as he limped toward his desk and sat down heavily. "I know what he wants to do. What I *don't* know is why I have to find out these details from other people when I should be hearing it directly from him."

"It's hard to talk to you when we only see you coming or going. Even Betty is complaining." Betty was his part-time nurse and had been with him since he'd first opened his practice.

"Don't you people have telephones? All you have to do is call."

"I've tried to reach you every night, like I always used to, and can't." It had been part of her routine to check on him around eight, but now she was rarely successful. Obviously, he didn't want to talk to her and the idea troubled her. But what could she do? She'd already explained, apologized and coaxed until she'd memorized every word. Backing off had been her only option.

She continued, "The three of us can't discuss plans and make decisions over the phone. Gavin has some good ideas—"

"He can keep his ideas to himself," Oliver said, opening the bottom drawer and resting his right foot on it. "This is still my practice and I have the final say on what goes on."

"Then you need to be here," she said firmly. "You may not have noticed, but we're as busy as ever."

"I knew Sinclair wouldn't pull his weight," Oliver said with satisfaction.

His attitude irritated her and she held onto her temper with supreme effort. "Gavin isn't the problem. Our patient list is growing. Most of Dr Stafford's clients are coming to us, especially those who couldn't find a physician after he retired. Rumors of Dr Dawson's impending retirement are bringing the others. Our waiting room is bursting at the seams at any given moment, which is why we have to think ahead."

He raised one bushy eyebrow. "Oh?"

"Izzie needs help. She can't keep up with the phones, the filing or processing the insurance claims."

"If she'd stop gabbing with everyone, she'd have plenty of time to do her work," he grumbled.

"You're not being fair, and you know it," she chided gently. "Izzie already does the job of two people—you've said so more than once."

"Fine," he snapped. "Let her hire someone. Part time."

"I'll tell her," she said. "Now, let me take a peek at your foot."

"It's nothing. I'm a doctor and I can take care of my own toe without getting a second opinion."

Knowing how foot problems and diabetes traveled hand in hand, Aly wasn't convinced. He also seemed shakier than usual, which concerned her. "All right. I'll check your blood sugar instead."

"I checked it before I left home."

"And?"

"It was a little high."

"How high is a little high?"

He mumbled, but she heard anyway. "Two forty-nine."

The normal glucose was slightly above a hundred. "Your idea of 'a little' is different than mine."

"I've been adjusting my dosage these past few weeks and I haven't hit on the right combination," he defended himself.

"It doesn't help when you sneak in a few cupcakes and an occasional piece of pie either." She smiled at his startled glance. "You're not the only one who hears gossip."

"It's gotten so a man can't sneeze without someone knowing about it," he groused.

"Not in Hartwell. Come on. Off with the shoe."

He glared at her but obeyed. Aly crouched to tug off his sock and as she saw his foot she inwardly groaned. His skin was white and cool to touch, and his big toe was swollen. Colored fluid oozed from around the blackened nail, which would probably fall off in a few days. Her practiced eye detected faint streaks of red radiating outward.

"What happened?"

"I stubbed my toe on the edge of my bed a week ago," he grumbled.

Guilt rose up within her. If she hadn't left him to his own devices, if she'd forced her way inside his house, perhaps she could have minimized the effects of his injury.

She glanced at her uncle. "Why didn't you tell me about this sooner? Surely you can see what I'm seeing."

"I can take care of myself. For your information, I've already started myself on antibiotics."

"Good. And you know that infections require adjustments to your insulin."

"I didn't graduate from medical school yesterday."

She ignored his sarcasm. "Don't move. I'll get my supplies."

"I'm not going anywhere. If you see Sinclair—"

"I'll send him in."

On her way back, with her arms laden with ointments and bandages, she ran into Gavin in the hallway. "Oliver wants to talk to you."

"Then we're even," he said wryly.

"He's not in a good mood," she warned.

He shrugged, as if it was inconsequential. Then again,

her uncle's short temper wasn't unusual. If only Gavin could see Oliver's other, more caring side.

Gavin accompanied her into Oliver's office. A characteristic glint that foretold of imminent fireworks shone in both men's eyes and she was glad to have an excuse for being present. The two would need a referee before this meeting ended.

"I'll work while you two talk," she informed her uncle.

Gavin moved closer to stare down at her while she swabbed her uncle's infected toe. "What's wrong?" he asked.

"I didn't ask you in here to discuss my foot," Oliver snapped. "I want to know why you're running all these tests on Laura Meadows."

Aly glanced up at Gavin and shrugged in response to the question in his eyes. She didn't have any idea how Oliver knew about Laura seeking out Gavin and hoped that he wouldn't hold her responsible.

"I overheard it at the coffee-shop," Oliver went on. "Two of Laura's friends were discussing how the new doctor in town is running her through the proverbial mill."

"I'm trying to determine the cause for her fatigue," he answered.

"She's tired from chasing after her husband and two kids. A vacation will take care of her problem but they don't have the money. They'll have even less by the time they get the bill for all of your tests."

"A vacation isn't the answer."

Oliver shook his head. "I've seen this before. You're not going to find anything."

"Maybe not, but I can't stop until I'm certain."

"You mean you're not going to stop until you've spent their kids' college fund."

"Gavin won't do that," Aly broke in.

"I'm only being thorough," Gavin insisted.

"Hah. Frivolous is more like it. I also want to know what nonsense you're starting at the hospital. You should have talked to me first."

Aly interrupted. "I've already explained why he didn't."

"I didn't ask you, Aly. I asked Sinclair."

Shocked by her uncle's reprimand, she glanced at Gavin. The tension in his jaw was obvious but he spoke evenly. "I tried, but you weren't available."

"You didn't try hard enough. Do you know how foolish I appear when people ask me questions and I don't know what my own colleague plans to do?"

"I only talked to the lab about adding some additional tests to their menu."

"Like what?" Oliver barked.

"I want the hemoglobin A1C testing done here at our hospital for faster results."

Measuring the hemoglobin A1C was vital to managing the long-term care of a diabetic. All too often, these patients would come in for a check-up and have a normal blood sugar, but the hemoglobin A1C test would be high, indicating that they hadn't maintained normal levels throughout the past month.

"That's a good idea," Aly interjected.

Both men ignored her, although Oliver grunted as she wrapped his toe. "Go easy, will you?" he told her before he attacked Gavin again. "What about the X-ray situation? We've sent our films to Guymon for years to be read. Why isn't that arrangement good enough for you?"

"It isn't a question of being good enough," Gavin explained. "It's more a case of improving what we already have in place."

"Bah!"

Gavin continued as if Oliver hadn't expressed his scorn. "I'd like to send the pictures to the radiologist over the internet so they can be read immediately, not three or four days later. A lot of small hospitals and clinics are already using the technology. We can also get the proper equipment to allow a specialist in another center to see a patient in our facility.''

Aly had heard of such capabilities, but the system had always seemed too far out of reach to implement under the current climate of limited medical reimbursements. Their hospital struggled to stay afloat without the additional expense of the latest bells and whistles, even if those advances had revolutionized medical care.

''Won't it cost a small fortune?'' she asked.

''Not as much as you think,'' Gavin answered. ''There are government grants we can apply for and I'm sure we can solicit donations.''

''It would be great to have a radiology report in a few hours instead of a few days.'' Aly was enthusiastic over the possibility. Although she and the doctors had learned to read the more simple films, they weren't specialists by any means and didn't pretend to be. ''You should be thanking Gavin for his forward thinking instead of yelling at him. If you recall, Pete wanted to bring us out of the medical Dark Ages.''

''Aly.'' Both men spoke at once.

''I do a solo,'' Oliver said sternly. ''If you can't keep quiet, leave.''

''But—'' she protested.

''Are you finished?'' Gavin asked, motioning to Oliver's foot.

''Yes.''

''Then I want to speak to you outside.''

She tried to stall. ''I have to clean up my mess.''

''Leave it.''

The tables had turned. In that instant, she'd lost her role as a go-between. She knew what she would hear once she left the room and she mentally prepared her defense as she slowly rose. Her uncle's expression remained as implacable as ever, so she would receive no help from that quarter. Squaring her shoulders, she brushed past Gavin to step into the hallway.

Gavin followed and closed the door. Immediately, she tried to explain. "I'm only trying to—"

"I know what you're doing, Aly, but Oliver is right. You're not helping matters."

She stared at him incredulously. How could he say that? Her current mission in life was to bring these two together. "I'm not helping?" she sputtered.

"No, you're not. I can speak for myself."

Her temper simmered. "Fine. If you two want scalpels at twenty paces, who am I to try and stop you?"

He rubbed the back of his neck. "Look, ever since I arrived, you've been organizing and orchestrating everything between Oliver and myself to suit your purposes."

She bristled. "Organizing? Orchestrating? Are you implying that I'm a control freak?"

"I'm not implying anything. The point is, I handle my own problems." She started to interrupt, but he wouldn't let her. "You once accused me of not allowing anyone else to help fight my battles. I remember. However, there are some battles that I have to fight myself."

"For example?"

"For example, the one with Oliver. We'll never work out our differences if you're always interfering."

"So now I'm interfering."

"Yes, you are. Tell me something, if your brothers got in an argument with their buddies, did your mother jump in and smooth things over?"

"No," she said slowly.

"That's right. They would have been laughed out of school. Plus, they would have been branded as mama's boys."

"This isn't the same."

"Isn't it?" His steely gaze didn't waver. "Every time something comes up that has the potential to be unpleasant, you wade in."

"I'm only trying to help." Heavens to Betsy, she was sounding like a parrot.

"I appreciate it, but you're not doing me any favors. Oliver and I have to find common ground for ourselves."

Instinctively, she knew he was right. She couldn't force Oliver to accept Gavin.

"I don't need you to be my mother, Aly. I want…"

His voice faded and her curiosity rose. "What? What do you want, Gavin?" Without any warning or indication of what was on his mind, Aly found herself grabbed by her upper arms.

"I want this," he said, before he lowered his mouth to hers.

The air left her lungs under his hard onslaught. Surprise slowly gave way to pleasure as his lips gentled and his tight grip dragged and held her against his frame.

Without warning, he released her. His gaze was intent as if he mentally willed her to understand what he couldn't explain in words. He didn't need to utter a single syllable. After those few seconds it took her brain to function again, she knew exactly what he wanted.

The prospect sent a flutter throughout her entire being. "I see," she said lamely.

With his expression inscrutable, and before she could string her tumbled thoughts together into something remotely coherent, he disappeared back into Oliver's office.

She watched him go, still reeling under the impact of his kiss. For a moment she wondered if she'd imagined the entire episode, but she hadn't because her lips still tingled.

He'd distanced himself from her before and she'd assumed her desire for him was one-sided. Apparently, *happily*, it wasn't.

Yet she couldn't help but wonder at his reaction. Surely after a couple shared a kiss, there would be a lingering touch, a shared smile, a whispered promise. Instead, he'd backed away without a word, as if he'd indulged a secret wish but hadn't been pleased by his actions.

Gavin Sinclair was definitely attracted to her but clearly didn't want to be. Before she could ponder it further, Izzie met her in the hallway.

"Well? What happened?"

Aly mentally shook herself out of her daze. "You can hire someone part time."

"Way to go, girl. I knew I could count on you. From the raised voices, I figured we didn't have a chance."

"That wasn't the problem."

"Then what was?"

Aly stared at the closed door as she listened intently for any noise that would tell her what was transpiring on the other side. "Oliver was raking Gavin over the coals."

"And you left them alone?"

"I didn't have much choice," she said wryly. "I was defending Gavin and the next thing I knew he'd escorted me outside." As she remembered, her irritation grew. "If those two want to butt heads like a pair of old goats, they can go at each other with my blessing."

"They're men. What can I say?" Izzie threw her hands in the air. "Then again, maybe they need to get physical. It would be one way to vent their pent-up energy."

Gavin's method of "getting physical" didn't bother Aly in the slightest. Now that she'd witnessed a crack in his iron-clad control, she hoped to see more of it drop away as time went on. With luck, incidents like that of a few minutes ago would occur again. Anticipation brought a hot flush to her face.

She drew a deep breath to calm herself. "You're right."

Izzie peered into Aly's face. "You look sort of strange. Are you OK?"

Aly managed a reassuring smile. "Sure. Why wouldn't I be?"

Izzie shrugged. "I don't know. You look different."

Of course she did, she thought wryly. Her entire world had shifted course. "I'm fine." She glanced at her watch to avoid meeting her receptionist's gaze. Gavin's kiss was too personal an event to share with anyone. The only way to throw Izzie off the scent was to return to business, which she did.

"How many patients are on my schedule this afternoon?"

"A few. Why? Are you going home early?"

She'd planned to, but now she didn't want to leave without talking to Gavin. Then again, broaching the subject of kissing while at work didn't appeal to her. The potential of being overheard was far too great.

"I haven't decided," she said. "I'm behind in my paperwork."

"Ah," Izzie said knowingly. "You want to hang around and see if any more fireworks develop."

"How did you guess?" Aly answered lightly.

"In case you've forgotten, you have school physicals tonight, too."

"Oh, yeah. Thanks for reminding me. You might say something to the others before they go home. They're so busy arguing, they probably won't remember either."

By the time she saw Gavin leaving Oliver's office, she had performed a well-baby check-up, removed the sutures she'd placed in Ed Jensen's hand a week ago and had rewritten a prescription for Sadie Redwing's blood-pressure medication.

As Gavin approached, he looked as if he wanted to say

something to her, but she was on her way into Mickey's room with five-year-old Heidi Johnson for a follow-up on her inner ear infection. His kiss was too fresh in her mind and meant too much for her to speak and act as if it had never occurred.

However, once Heidi began chattering, Aly wished that she hadn't seen Gavin at all.

"I'm wearing my Winnie-the-Pooh underwear today," the little girl said proudly. "I wanted to have Tweety Bird undies like you do, but Mama couldn't find any. Are you wearing Tweety Bird today?"

Feeling Gavin's attention focus on her, Aly wanted to slide into the cracks on the floor. "No, I'm not," she answered, wishing the child had never noticed those particular socks one day.

"You told me you always wear cartoon underwear," Heidi accused.

Aly inwardly groaned. "I only wear silly socks," she told the little girl in a tone loud enough for Gavin to hear. She wasn't about to describe the rest of her undergarments to a child. From the gleam in Gavin's eye, though, he clearly wouldn't object if she did. "Today isn't a Tweety Bird day."

"Then what day is it?"

"Snow White."

"Oh, I like her. Can I see?"

Gavin cleared his throat as if to stifle a chuckle. Hot from embarrassment, Aly hurried Heidi and her mother into the exam room. "I'll show you my feet after I look in your ears. OK?"

Heidi nodded her agreement and climbed onto the table with her mother's help.

"Any problems with the antibiotics?" Aly asked Mrs Johnson.

"None at all."

Aly held up the digital ear thermometer. Whoever had invented this method of taking temperatures rather than orally had earned her undying gratitude. "All right, half-pint. Hold still for me and then you can go home."

Heidi obeyed. In a few minutes, Aly had checked her ear canals with the otoscope and declared her fit.

"Your turn," Heidi declared.

Aly stood with one foot on the stool and raised her trouser leg. Heidi stared at the figures of Snow White dancing with her seven dwarfs and sighed with obvious delight. "Pretty," she said.

After dutifully admiring Heidi's socks, Aly sent mother and daughter on their way. Gavin was nowhere to be seen, which made her feel equal measures of disappointment and relief.

Her four o'clock and final appointment for the day arrived early. Emma Carothers had crippling arthritis and her current pain relief wasn't doing the job. Aly dispensed samples of a different medication and instructed her to report back with news of how this drug worked.

She lingered in her office, waiting for Gavin to appear, but the minutes ticked by. After finally asking Izzie his whereabouts, she learned that he'd been called to the hospital. The talk she wanted would have to wait.

In the meantime, her prediction had come to pass. Life at the clinic had certainly changed.

Gavin could see the impatience in Aly's eyes and the eagerness on her face the moment he walked into the high-school gymnasium filled with the hundred or so students who wanted to play sports and needed a physical to comply with the district's policy. He should have spoken to her before now, but he hadn't enjoyed a moment's peace since he'd left the clinic. What he had to say would require time and privacy, both of which were lacking at the moment.

He wasn't in any particular hurry to burst her bubble of happiness, but he would. He had no other choice. Regardless of how she'd burrowed into his heart in spite of his most determined efforts, he had to be firm. As much as he wanted it to be otherwise, there were too many strikes against them, more specifically against him, and her uncle ranked at the top of the list of obstacles.

He'd thought one kiss would force her out of his system, but it hadn't. Thoughts of another, and another, and still another teased him. One hadn't been enough and he'd been foolish to think it would. Now the memory would haunt him for ever.

Actually, he had two memories to plague him. The little girl who'd talked about Aly's underwear hadn't done him any favors. Aly might have only been talking about her socks, but he'd painted a very different mental picture.

He simply had to tell her that he hadn't meant anything by his kiss. It would be a mistake for her to read it as a romantic gesture. Personal relationships required a great deal of time and energy. He didn't have either and, from what he'd seen this past month, neither did she.

Between her career and looking after her mother and uncle, he'd wager a guess that she barely remembered what the inside of her home looked like. It was absolutely untenable to fall in love with someone who didn't have a moment's peace for herself. How would she have time for him, and vice versa? He was selfish enough to want more than crumbs in a relationship, and crumbs were all Aly had left to give.

Two hours later, Gavin scanned the medical checklist of the last fourteen-year-old student standing in front of him. ''What sport are you going to play?'' he asked the tall, gangly adolescent.

''Basketball.'' His voice ended on a squeak and his face turned a bright red.

"A great sport." Gavin placed his stethoscope against the boy's bare chest. "How are you at free throws?"

"I make ninety-five per cent," he boasted. "At camp this summer, Coach told us about how they were free points, so we had to learn how to make 'em. I've been practicing hard."

"If you're sinking that many, I'd say so." Gavin listened to the boy's heart and lungs. After performing a few more checks, he scrawled his name at the bottom of the medical record. "I'll be watching for your name in the newspaper, Keith. Have a great season."

"Thanks, Dr Sinclair."

As soon as Keith had left, Gavin gathered his stack of papers into a neat pile. He hadn't anticipated finding any undiagnosed medical problems and this group of kids had met his expectations. The only issue facing him now involved Aly, and she was headed in his direction with the athletic director in tow.

"I want to thank you for taking time out this evening for us," Dave Burkhart said.

"We were happy to come," Gavin answered. "From the looks of your students, you should have a fantastic basketball team. Hartwell has a lot of boys tall for their age."

"We do," Dave agreed. "I hope you'll take in a few of our games."

"I'm sure we will," Aly said.

After saying their goodbyes, Gavin walked outside with Aly into the cool evening air. It was eight o'clock and the sun hung over the horizon like a giant red beach-ball.

"Betty said you had a patient to see at the hospital."

So she'd checked on him. "A trucker passing through town came in with respiratory distress. His inhaler was outdated and he was wheezing. We ended up giving him prednisone with his albuterol."

"I waited for you."

He'd assumed she would. "We should talk about what happened today."

"Yes, we should. Your place or mine?"

He thought quickly. If he were going to upset Aly or drive her to tears, he'd rather not do it in the vicinity of her mother. "Yours."

"Have you eaten?" she asked.

"No."

"All right. We'll talk over dinner." She stopped beside her car and slid behind the wheel. "I'll see you in a few minutes."

For a split second he debated going home, but her voice had held a resolve that said she would hunt him down if he didn't appear on schedule. Truthfully, he'd rather avoid her completely. She wouldn't like hearing what he had to say and he only wanted to spare her feelings.

From the moment he arrived at her house, she touched on every subject but the most important one. He was selfish enough to follow her lead and delay what would surely be an awkward discussion. At least for the next half-hour, they would simply be two people enjoying each other's company.

For dessert, she served the best chocolate cake he'd ever eaten. "Did you make this?" he asked, savoring each bite.

"Last night. Do you like it?"

"Is it hot in the summer? Of course I like it." He swallowed another bite. "You're going to make some man very happy if he has food like this waiting for him every night."

She smiled. "I hope so. The question is, are you that man?"

CHAPTER EIGHT

GAVIN slowly placed his fork on his plate. Although Aly had spoken lightly, he sensed it hadn't been an idle question. "I can't be the man you want," he answered flatly.

She rested both elbows on the table and leaned forward. "Why not?"

He stared at her incredulously. "You're asking me why not? Isn't it obvious?"

"Not to me."

"There are too many roadblocks."

"Like what?"

"Come on, Aly. Get serious."

"I am. What are these roadblocks you're talking about?"

"Your uncle, for one."

Her sculpted eyebrows drew together. "What does Oliver have to do with us being attracted to each other?"

Hearing her admit to the same feelings as his for her gave him a momentary sense of pride...and joyful relief. Those emotions, however, were soon wiped away as common sense took control. "Nothing, but—"

"See?" she said triumphantly. "What we feel for each other is strictly between us."

He shook his head. "No, it isn't. Your relatives play a part whether you want to admit it or not. It's always been that way."

"I suppose you're right," she said thoughtfully. "Look at Romeo and Juliet."

He would hardly have described their situation in terms of the romantic pair, but at least she understood the point he was trying to make. Family support was crucial. "Ex-

134

actly. Your uncle barely tolerates me in his clinic. Do you really think he'd willingly accept me as more than a colleague?''

"You're giving up too easily."

"I'm being realistic," he corrected.

"Oliver won't interfere in my private life," she insisted.

He sat back and folded his arms. "Would you care to make a small wager?''

"He wants me to be happy."

"I'm sure he does." But not with me, he finished silently.

"I've said it before and I'll say it again. You're giving up too easily." He opened his mouth to speak, but she held up her hands. "However, I'll let this argument rest for the time being. I want to hear about these other roadblocks you think we have in our way.''

"Neither of us have time for a relationship."

"We don't?"

Gavin shook his head again. "I'm committed to medicine. It's my whole life. It's why I came.''

"So you came out of an obligation to Pete. I'm sure he wouldn't expect you to spend every waking moment with a stethoscope around your neck. My profession is important to me, too, but it doesn't completely define my existence. I intend to have a life that has room for family reunions, PTA meetings, school concerts and Little League games.''

"From what your mother tells me, you don't."

"That was before you arrived. In case you haven't noticed, my nieces and nephew are still too young for all of those activities," she said with a grin. "Yes, I've been pressed for time. Working and studying toward another nursing degree doesn't happen overnight. The good thing is that with our load divided three ways instead of two, we can all develop outside interests.''

"I'm not complaining, but in case you haven't realized

it, you and I carry nearly eighty per cent of this practice. That's nearly half for each of us, which translates into either you or I working every night. Then there are those patients who need more than you are able to provide. We'd *both* be working. How would we possibly spend meaningful time together?''

"Other couples manage."

Remembering his childhood, he wasn't convinced. His parents had rarely been at home and when they had been, they'd rarely remained in the same room. ''Do they?''

"Of course they do. We might have to juggle our schedules but it can be done. My mother would love to watch the kids—''

"Children?" How had they made the jump from spending time together to children?

Aly shrugged. ''You're obviously looking down the road at every possible hurdle we'd have to face, so I thought I'd nip that objection in the bud. Don't you want children?''

"Yes, but you're already exhausted with the pace you've set for yourself. Between looking after your mom and your uncle, you hardly have any extra energy now, much less if you add a husband and kids to the equation.''

"For the record," she said mildly, ''I didn't set this pace for myself. I fell into it because I didn't have any other choice. Believe me, I'll be just as happy slowing down so I can stop and smell the honeysuckle along the way.''

From the day he'd met her, Gavin had been struck by her willingness to indulge in quiet pursuits like fishing and walking through the park. He would have expected someone with her bubbly personality and natural optimism to prefer being the center of attention, but she'd seemed just as happy when a bystander as she had when she'd been an active participant. By her own admission, those opportunities to watch the world go by hadn't come as frequently as she would have liked these past few years.

A knowing expression appeared on Aly's face. "This is what you're worried about, isn't it? That I won't find time for you?"

Surprised and startled by her insight, Gavin drew a ragged breath. "I'm only pointing out that you've been running yourself ragged. Between your practice and looking after the family you already have, you don't have anything left for anyone else."

Her calm, placid demeanor suddenly shifted to indignation. She rose regally and skirted the table to stand next to him. "I'll have you know," she said as she poked his shoulder with each word, "I *make* the time for the people and things I consider important. And don't you forget it."

Stunned, he watched her and felt an undefined emotion unfurl inside him. Was it conceivable to believe that if she placed him in the same "important" category then maybe, just maybe, his life wouldn't become a carbon copy of his parents'? He wanted the idea to be true, but at the same time he wasn't prepared to test it. At least, not yet.

Suddenly, she heaved a deep sigh, then leaned one hip against the table. "This all is such a horrible waste."

"A waste? What do you mean?"

"It's a waste for me. For both of us."

"I don't follow you."

She answered with a smile, "I shouldn't tell you this because it will probably go to your head, but you're an extremely attractive man. When Pete brought you here three years ago and I met you for the first time, it was as if every guy I'd ever dated paled in comparison. As far as I was concerned, we simply clicked, like two halves of a whole. We shared tastes in music, in spicy food and even in the way we both liked to sit on the porch and watch the sun set. I'd never been with a guy who matched me so perfectly and I could hardly wait for you to finish your residency. I dreamed big dreams."

Gavin hardly knew what to say. He'd felt that connection as well. He'd been thrilled to join forces with Pete, but he'd savored the prospect of seeing Aly on a daily basis. A practice in Hartwell, with all its challenges, was like an ice-cream sundae, and Aly was the crowning touch.

"And then you left town," she continued.

"Because you and Oliver told me to go," he reminded her.

"I didn't know what to do. Everything fell apart and I was left scrambling to pull the pieces back together. Mom was a wreck and Oliver was…well, you know how he was. I tried phoning you, but you never answered or returned my calls."

He winced as he remembered. At the time, it had seemed for the best. In retrospect, it hadn't been.

"I knew you were hurting, but I'd hoped our mutual loss would draw us together."

"So you kept calling."

Her smile was tender. "Month after month, I tried to reach you, until one day I spoke to your roommate. I can't remember his name. Jake, or Jerry, or—"

"John," he supplied.

She shrugged, as if his identity wasn't important. "He told me that you'd gone to a party with Ginger and wouldn't be home until late the next day. At that moment, I realized what I'd begun to suspect but would never admit. You'd found someone else, or that someone else had found you." Her chuckle sounded weak. "I was so jealous of her. She'd landed the most handsome fellow in the world and I was green with envy. I was even angrier with you. After that, I did my best to forget your phone number."

So that explained why her calls had come to an abrupt end. "Ginger was a fellow resident. She wanted someone to escort her to her sister's engagement party in Dallas."

"Then she wasn't your girlfriend?"

Gavin shook his head. "She had her heart set on a Marine. As much as I liked her, I wasn't about to tangle with him since he appeared quite capable of snapping me in two with his bare hands. They've since married."

"I'm glad."

"That I didn't tangle with a Marine or that she's married?" he teased.

She laughed. "Both. Now that I know my feelings aren't one-sided, I think we should see what, if anything, develops."

"Wait a minute—"

Aly interrupted. "Did you or did you not kiss me like you wanted more than a stolen kiss?"

Just thinking about her in his arms sent his blood pressure up a few points. Knowing they were alone, without any chance of someone walking in unannounced, raised it several more. "I did."

"Then call it sparks, electricity, whatever. It's our duty to let nature take its course."

"Our duty?" he echoed.

"If we're meant for each other, I'd hate for you to spend the rest of your life making someone else miserable."

He laughed at her convoluted thinking and the impish gleam in her eyes. "Your logic astounds me."

She grinned. "It should. Anyway, I know you're worried and wary of what lies ahead. Maybe for us, nothing does. Don't we owe it to ourselves to find out?"

Her argument sounded very persuasive but, then, perhaps it was because in one area of his heart he wanted to do exactly as she'd said.

She leaned closer. "Tell me I've misread the situation. Say that you're not interested in me any more than you are in Ginger. Put your what ifs and your logic on hold and tell me what you feel."

Aly pressed her mouth to his and he was lost. Her lips

were soft, her scent tantalizing and her skin as smooth as silk. More importantly, she was too far away to suit him.

He gripped her arms and pulled her off balance, guiding her onto his lap. Once there, he folded his arms around her and let himself fall under the magical spell she'd woven around him.

The rest of the world faded to black as he focused his complete and undivided attention on her. He'd kissed women before, but not like this where he actually entertained thoughts and dreams of a future. The few women he'd gone out with knew he hadn't been offering more than a night or two of simple companionship, and they'd accepted those limitations.

Aly, however, was the absolute opposite. With her, one night couldn't begin to be enough. Two were barely an appetizer. Only a lifetime could come close to being enough, although even that seemed far too short. Something consumed him, some emotion he hadn't experienced before. Whatever it was, it swept through him with all the ferocity of a forest fire.

Her body pressed against his as he accepted her slight weight. His fingers took on a will of their own, charting every curve and every valley of her lovely form. For what it was worth, he regretted the pain he'd caused her. Undoing the past wasn't possible, but he slowly felt her optimism for the future sink into his empty spaces until her unfailing faith in happy endings suddenly became contagious. Slaying dragons seemed like child's play. No problem seemed insurmountable.

Nothing except her family.

He'd wanted to be included in that small select circle from the moment he'd first set foot in this small community. Now she was hanging the prize within reach, but the possibility of rejection was too great for him to grab the dream with both hands. One question haunted him. If she had to choose, where would he stand in her affections? In first place, or a distant second?

Somehow Gavin managed to pull his mouth away, although he wasn't ready to let her go.

"As much as I want this, it would never work," he said slowly. "Your uncle won't stand for it."

Aly stiffened in his arms. "This is about us. You and me. Oliver isn't a part of this."

"He is," he insisted.

Aly twisted in his arms to stare at him, her eyes narrowed. "What did he say this afternoon?"

"What I'd expected. That he wanted to know what I was doing before I did it." Gavin didn't mention how he'd reminded Oliver that he was a qualified physician and as such would continue to ask the various hospital departments to improve their services as he saw fit. Actually, by the time they'd parted company, he'd soothed Oliver's ruffled feathers to the point where the older man had been almost civil.

"He's also agreed to dedicate an hour where the four of us, Izzie included, can discuss problems, concerns and possible improvements."

Her face brightened. "Then you made progress."

"In a manner of speaking. I've been thinking, though. Wouldn't it be great if we could turn one wing of the hospital into a diagnostic center? We could name it after Pete."

"That would be wonderful. Did you mention it to Oliver?"

"Not yet. I don't want to hit him with too many things at once. Besides, this idea is still on the drawing board."

"I hope we can bring it to pass," she said. "So, what else did Oliver say?"

"He didn't warn me to keep my hands off you, if that's what you're asking."

"Then what are you worried about?"

"Because once the thought crosses his mind, that's exactly what he'll tell me. And we'll end up heading in separate directions." Again, he finished silently. And this time he'd find it much harder to pick up the pieces and move on.

"Stop being so negative. If I'd concentrated on every potential problem associated with bringing you here, I would never have tracked you down in the first place. You have to think positively."

"Wanting something badly enough won't make it happen," he told her. "You were lucky."

"I'm tenacious," she corrected. "In case you've forgotten your history, a famous military strategy is to divide and conquer. If we're united, nothing can tear us apart."

In theory, Gavin agreed. In practice, however, he wasn't as certain. "I want to believe you, but..."

Aly understood his doubt. The wounds he'd sustained from both his family and hers were too great for her to expect instant healing from a few reassurances. She was, however, a patient woman.

She slipped off his lap. "Anything worth having is worth fighting for. I think that what we could have falls into that category. Don't you?"

"Then you're not still angry with me?"

She squeezed his hand. "I stopped the Sunday that I kissed you. Now, let's take each day as it comes and deal with the problems if and when they appear."

"All right."

Aly wondered if Gavin had realized how quickly folks would draw their own conclusions if they saw them together during their off-duty hours. Hartwell didn't provide the same anonymity to its citizens as Oklahoma City did. While she didn't mind if everyone knew the newest doctor was romancing the community's nurse-practitioner, Gavin would. Until he regained his confidence in her, she didn't want to do anything that could jeopardize their budding relationship.

"Since we've settled that," she asked coyly, "shall we sit outside and do a little star-gazing?"

"There's nothing wrong with my view from here," he said as he stared into her eyes.

She blushed, but before she could answer, her pager sounded. "So much for a quiet evening," she mourned.

"Who's calling?"

She glanced at the display. "The hospital. Let me see what they want." A minute and a phone call later, she knew.

"I've got to go," she said reluctantly. "Can we get together later?"

"Sure. Call me when you're free."

She smiled. "Aren't you glad your apartment has a separate entrance?"

"More than you know." He followed her outside to her car. "See you soon."

"Soon" came more quickly than she'd expected. Less than an hour later, she summoned him to the ER.

"I'm sorry to call you out," she apologized, "but I have a nineteen-year-old college girl with a low-grade fever, headache and malaise. In the short time I've seen her, she's shown a distinct intolerance to light, some confusion and twitching."

"What about Kernig's signs?"

The test he'd mentioned was a basic procedure used to determine meningeal irritation. It involved flexing the head and legs to different degrees, thereby stretching the various types of connective tissue that lined the brain and encased the spinal cord. Any resultant muscle spasms indicated the presence of inflammation.

"Both are positive. I've never seen the textbook petechial rash before, but now I have." She was referring to a red rash that appeared on the lower portion of the body and was a result of pinpoint bleeding into the skin because of broken capillaries.

"Where's she been going to school?"

Because she knew the family quite well, Aly was able to answer. "At a community college in Kansas. Dodge City, to be exact. Apparently a friend drove her home. She wouldn't have made it here otherwise."

"What's her white count?"

Aly handed the lab report to him. "It's over three times normal at thirty-five thousand. There's also a definite shift to the left," she said, referring to the presence of immature cells. "And her electrolytes are out of whack."

He scanned the page. "So I see. As far as I can tell, your diagnosis is on the right track. Shall we do the LP?"

She glowed under his praise. "Everything's ready. We were waiting for a doctor."

"Then let's not waste any more time. Are her parents still here?"

"Yes. Their names are Gary and Ann Whitlow. Joy is their eldest."

Aly led the way to the trauma room and introduced Gavin to the Whitlows as they stood on either side of Joy's hospital bed, clutching her hands. Even though the nurses had dimmed the lights to make Joy more comfortable, the worry on Gary's and Ann's faces was more than evident.

"We think Joy may have meningitis," Gavin told them in a low voice. "We're going to do a spinal tap to know for certain."

"But I thought only children and babies got meningitis," Ann said in a near-frantic voice.

"They have a higher risk," Gavin admitted, "but the disease is no respecter of persons. I've seen young and old alike contract the disease. Anywhere there's a large group of people living together, there's an increased risk."

"Like in college dormitories?" Gary asked.

Gavin nodded. "University students and military recruits are especially susceptible. There are vaccines now to minimize the risk, but not everyone gets immunized. How long has she been ill?"

"She called at the end of last week to tell us she'd gone to the campus health department because of a sinus infection. They prescribed an antibiotic, but I don't know what it was," Ann said. "I think she brought the bottle home with her, though."

"It would be helpful if you can tell us what she was taking," Gavin said.

"I'll have her sister look for those pills right away," Ann promised. "Doctor? If she has…meningitis, will she…be OK? I mean, I've heard of stories of deafness and neurological problems and…and…" She stopped as if she couldn't speak her fears aloud.

"The sooner we start treatment," Gavin said kindly, "the better for Joy. If we can get her through these next few hours seizure-free, that's a good sign. Now, if you two will step outside, we'll get things rolling."

Ann bent over her daughter to kiss her cheek and smooth the hair off her forehead. Gary pressed his lips to Joy's hand before he placed it back on the bed. "Come on, Mother," he said gruffly to Ann.

"As soon as we're finished, you can sit with her," Aly said.

The couple nodded and left. While Aly and the ER nurse arranged their supplies for a lumbar puncture and maneuvered Joy into a curled position in order to increase the space between the vertebrae, Gavin gowned. After sterilizing the area, Gavin inserted the needle, took a pressure reading and then allowed the precious fluid to drip into sterile tubes.

Aly focused her attention on the small vials. From her

position, she could see the specimen's cloudy appearance, which wasn't a good sign. Normal spinal fluid was clear and colorless, like water.

He handed the first vial to her. "I want a cell count, protein, glucose, culture and a gram stain, stat. And see if the lab have received their new kit to screen for bacterial antigens."

"Will do."

"Have we taken blood cultures?" he asked.

"Not yet," Aly said.

"I want two sets drawn as soon as we're done."

By the time they'd finished, the lab tech had arrived and was waiting to whisk the tubes away.

"I don't want to wait for the reports before we begin treatment," he told Aly and the other nurse. "It may be an hour or more until we have our answers and we can't afford to give the bacteria more of a head start than it already has. Is she allergic to penicillin?"

"Not according to her parents."

"Then we'll use penicillin, twenty-four million units in divided doses every four hours." He added his orders for mannitol, an osmotic diuretic which would decrease the amount of cerebral edema, an anticonvulsant to control her involuntary movements and acetaminophen to reduce her fever and relieve her headache. Seizure activity was a common symptom of intracranial pressure and minimizing that was of prime concern. Her electrolyte balance also had to be restored but without causing fluid overload, which would worsen the cerebral edema.

All in all, administering the necessary medication was a delicate balancing act for the physician and required alert nursing personnel.

"Find a bed in ICU for her," he instructed. "I want her vital signs closely watched and seizure precautions put into place. Let's get her temp down."

While Aly and the nurse worked to implement his orders, Gavin updated Joy's parents as they stood near the doorway. "Joy's spinal fluid was cloudy, so I'm fairly certain about the diagnosis. We're starting the large doses of antibiotic and we're moving her to ICU where she can be monitored around the clock."

"How will we know if what you're doing is working?" Gary asked.

"Her temperature will drop. It may be twenty-four hours or so before we see any significant changes," he cautioned. "We're using a broad-spectrum antibiotic, but once we know for certain what bug we're dealing with and what it's susceptible to, we may change our therapy."

"Can we stay with her?" Ann asked. "I know ICU doesn't allow visitors, but we won't get in the way."

Aly glanced at Gavin, wondering how he'd respond to her plea.

"If she doesn't worsen over the next few hours, I don't see why one of you can't stay with her. The rooms aren't very big and the staff will constantly be going in and out, so I can't let you both be there at the same time. If her condition changes, you'll have to leave."

"We understand."

Soon a nurse from ICU arrived and within thirty minutes Aly, Gavin and the intensive care staff had Joy ensconced in a glassed-in cubicle near the center of the ward and hooked to a variety of monitors to keep tabs on her heart rate and respirations.

While the unit's nurses began the first of what would be many assessments, Gavin and Aly returned to the central nurses' station. "Any word from the lab?" he asked.

Aly shook her head. "It's too soon."

"Did you find out if they can run a bacterial antigen screen?"

She knew it was a test where the fluid was mixed with

a solution of antibodies to the various bacteria that were commonly associated with meningitis. A positive result indicated the bug's identity without waiting twenty-four hours for a culture to grow the micro-organism.

"The kit is in but, according to the tech, they're not ready to use it on patients."

He frowned. "Pass the phone." Within moments, he had the lab supervisor on the other line. "Tom? I hear you have the test kit I'd requested, but you can't use it."

Aly listened shamelessly to the one-sided conversation.

"Well, if you can't give me an official result, can I at least have an *unofficial* one?" He fell silent for a few seconds before he said, "Thanks, Tom. I really appreciate it." He dropped the receiver back in its cradle and looked quite pleased with himself.

"Are they going to do the test?" Aly asked, amazed at how easily he'd gotten what he wanted.

"Yeah. They apparently have to run a certain number of known negative and positive samples to meet the requirements for bringing new procedures on board. Until then they can't document their result, but with luck their answer will match the reference lab's. Between this test and the gram stain, we should know if we're on the right track before long. If it isn't meningococcus, I'll owe you a drink."

"You're on," she said. "As long as it's not coffee."

He smiled. "What would you prefer?"

"A glass of Chardonnay."

He smiled. "I like a woman who knows what she wants."

"And don't you forget it."

The ICU nurse assigned to Joy approached. "Her temp is still elevated at one hundred three point five."

"Start sponging her down," he ordered.

The nurse obeyed and another thirty minutes ticked by.

"Where are those reports?" Gavin demanded. It wasn't terribly late—about ten o'clock—but waiting wasn't an easy job.

"It shouldn't be much longer," Aly soothed.

At that moment, the telephone jangled and Gavin snatched up the receiver on the first ring. "Sinclair," he barked.

Aly watched him listen intently, his face impassive. Finally, he said, "Thanks." And hung up.

"Well?" she demanded.

A slow grin spread across his face. "Intracellular gram-negative diplococci, and the antigen screen was positive for *Neisseria meningitidis*."

"You were right. I guess that means I won't get my glass of wine."

He grinned. "I could be persuaded to buy you one anyway."

"Could you?"

"Sure. Provided I had the proper incentive."

She flashed him a come-hither smile. "I think that can easily be arranged. We'll have to postpone it until Oliver is on call, though."

"True." He stood and stretched. "I'll walk you to your car."

Aly glanced at the young woman lying so still on the hospital bed, hearing the steady blips of the monitor in the background. "I'll hang around for awhile. Just in case."

"They'll notify us if there's any change. You might as well get some rest while you can."

She shrugged. "I know. I will. I need to stay for a little longer. An hour or so."

"Do you always do this?"

"Do I always do what?"

"Hang around longer than you need to. Wearing yourself out now won't help her or your other patients tomorrow."

"I know. I just can't leave."

He nodded. "I used to be the same way in med school. I soon learned that tiring myself out didn't do anyone any good."

She sighed because he sounded like Oliver. "You're not telling me what I don't already know. It's just that Joy was one of the first kids I babysat as a teenager. I can't go home. If I did, I wouldn't sleep anyway." Meeting his gaze, she willed him to understand.

As if he knew his arguments would fall on deaf ears, he shrugged. "The doctors' lounge has a spare bed and sofa. We'll both stay for a few hours and grab a few winks."

"You can go home."

"I could," he agreed, "but I have this feeling that if I don't keep an eye on you, I'll find you in this chair in the morning."

Aly grinned at how accurately he'd pegged her.

"Come on," he coaxed. "Let the nurses do their job. If we need to, we can get here in a heartbeat."

The thought of closing her eyes for a short time sounded very good after a busy and emotionally harrowing day. "All right. I'll tell them where to find us."

A few minutes later, Gavin guided her toward the bed in the inner sanctum of the physicians' private lounge, but she detoured toward the sofa. "I'm shorter than you are," she said. "Sleep tight."

He pulled her close. "This wasn't how I thought the night would end."

Aly smiled. "Same here."

"Do you see how tough it will be for us?"

She saw it far more clearly than she wanted to admit. Being forced to live on stolen moments wasn't how she envisioned their future. "Nothing good comes easy," she commented as much for herself as for him. "It will get better. 'Where there's a will, there's a way'."

"Are you always going to quote those tired old sayings?"

"Only when they're appropriate," she responded promptly.

He shook his head with amusement before he released her. "Get some sleep."

"What? No goodnight kiss?"

He moved toward the bed. "If I did, neither of us would get any rest. More importantly, I'd rather not be interrupted." A feral grin spread across his face. "I want us to take our time so we get it right. If you know what I mean."

An evening when they could enjoy each other at a leisurely pace sounded like pure heaven. "My sentiments exactly."

CHAPTER NINE

ALY slept from midnight until four, at which time she tip-toed from the lounge. Gavin had looked so peaceful as he sprawled across the bed but he wouldn't be happy to learn that her own rest had been short-lived. He might have perfected the ability to snooze wherever and whenever, but she hadn't.

"How's she doing?" she asked one of the ICU night nurses as she glanced at the only active monitor out of several on the desk.

"No real change. It's almost time to check her vitals again."

Wanting to see for herself, Aly followed the nurse into Joy's cubicle. The steady rise and fall of Joy's chest and the rhythmic blips flowing across the screen confirmed the nurse's report.

"How is she?" Ann asked in a low voice.

"Holding her own," Aly answered.

"I'd hoped to see some improvement."

"She isn't any worse. That's an accomplishment in itself."

Ann sighed. "I know. I can hardly believe how fast and how sick a person can get. It's frightening to watch her lie there so quietly. She never could sit still, even when she was sleeping."

"I remember," Aly said wryly, recalling how she'd drag herself home after an evening spent with Joy. If the little girl with the endearing blond curls hadn't been such a happy, inquisitive child, Aly would never have gone back time after time. "Seeing her like this is a shock, but all her energy is focused on fighting the infection. Be glad you brought her into the ER when you did. A few hours later would have made a tremendous difference.''

''I know. I shudder whenever I think about it. If I'd known she was this ill, I would have told her to go to the hospital in Dodge City instead of coming home.''

''You didn't, so don't blame yourself.''

Ann rose to gaze down at her daughter. ''I've been sitting here remembering how you looked after her whenever Gary and I splurged on an evening out for just the two of us. I never dreamed that you'd still do it when she was an adult. You saved her life.''

''Dr Sinclair did all the work,'' she said modestly.

''Maybe, but it helps me to know that you're watching over her, too.''

''I appreciate the vote of confidence. Don't expect any real change until tonight or even tomorrow,'' Aly cautioned.

''I realize that, but have you ever wanted something so badly that you could hardly contain yourself?''

Aly grinned. ''More often than you can imagine.''

Ann's voice grew distant. ''She was so excited when she received her volleyball scholarship. If she isn't able to play…''

''Joy may come out of this perfectly fine. Don't look for trouble. It has its own way of finding you.''

''You're right.'' Ann cleared her throat. ''Do you suppose anyone else at the college will catch meningitis from her?''

''I hope not,'' Aly said fervently, thinking of how easily the scenario could become a public health nightmare. ''We'll notify the campus authorities as soon as possible. The staff will locate her close contacts, like her roommates or a boyfriend, so they can receive prophylactic treatment. Your own family needs it as well.''

"She wasn't home that long before we brought her to the ER."

"It doesn't matter. If she sneezed or coughed, you may be exposed. Drop by the clinic this morning and I'll start you all on a dose of rifampin."

"We'll be there."

The nurse finished her checks and straightened the sheets. "No change," she said.

Ann inhaled a shaky breath and Aly patted her shoulder. "No change is better than if she gets worse. Remember that."

"I'll try."

Aly turned to go. "I'll drop in later this morning, so will Dr Sinclair."

"I appreciate it."

At five, she made her way to the doctors' lounge where she found Gavin seated on the edge of the bed, looking dangerously handsome with an early morning shadow covering his face. "How long have you been gone?" he asked.

"About an hour."

"How is she?"

"The same. I was going to run home and shower. After I woke you, of course." She grinned. "The diner opens for breakfast in an hour. Want to meet me there? Or would you rather drop by my place for scrambled eggs?"

"Scrambled eggs sound good."

She'd hoped he would choose her cooking. Not because she was a great chef, but because they would have privacy. "See you then."

Aly hurried home, showered away the lingering cobwebs and slipped into a fresh scrub suit. It wasn't until she tugged on her socks that she realized what she'd subconsciously chosen to wear. Both her socks and her tunic were covered in hearts of every shape, size and color, and it wasn't remotely close to Valentine's Day.

Even if it had been, the magnitude of her feelings for Gavin caught her by surprise. So much for her speech about wanting to see if they could possibly have a relationship. She'd gone and fallen in love with him.

Hugging her new-found knowledge to herself, she hurried into the kitchen and began whipping the eggs and chopping fresh vegetables. By the time the coffee-maker had sputtered its last drip and the eggs were done to a turn, Gavin arrived, looking fresh in his crisply pressed beige-colored trousers and red polo shirt.

"It smells delicious," he commented.

Watching him make himself at home in her kitchen, Aly wanted to tell him how she felt. Being as cautious as he was, though, he would run in the opposite direction. Instead, she spooned his serving onto a plate. "I hope it tastes the same."

"Why wouldn't it?"

"I tend to throw things together."

He eyed the plate suspiciously. "You didn't put anything weird in here, did you?"

"What do you consider weird?"

"Anchovies. Mushrooms."

"No fish and no fungi," she reassured him. "So dig in."

The next hour flew by. When Gavin left to make his morning hospital rounds, she could hardly wait to see him again at their medical offices. She was pathetic, she decided with a giggle, but she was too happy to care.

"The last of your test results arrived," Gavin told Laura Meadows later that same afternoon.

She gave him a tired smile. "So what have you decided that I *don't* have?"

"No Lyme disease."

"For supposedly being so healthy, I certainly feel awful. So what's next?"

"We've ruled everything out that we possibly can," he said carefully. "It's my opinion that you have chronic fatigue syndrome."

She frowned. "I've never heard of it."

"CFS is basically a catch-all phrase for your symptoms. Researchers haven't been able to discover a root cause, although some believe it's due to some sort of inflammatory process involving the central nervous system."

"Then how do I get rid of it?"

"There are some new antiviral agents in clinical trials right now, and if you'd like, I can try to enroll you in those studies. However, there are no guarantees that these drugs will work. All I can do is give you supportive care until your own immune system fights back."

"What do you mean by supportive care?"

"We basically try to minimize the side-effects, which is what we're already doing to a certain degree. For example, you reported having trouble sleeping and feeling depressed. I can prescribe something to help you with those particular symptoms. Meanwhile, you should continue taking the non-steroidal anti-inflammatory for your muscle pain."

"How long will it take until I'm back to normal? Or at least to what *used* to be normal?"

"I wish I could give you a firm date, but I can't," Gavin said ruefully. "Recovery time varies from months to years."

"That's not particularly promising," she said dryly.

"I know, but the very worst thing you can do is to lie around and do nothing. Studies have shown that those who stayed as active as possible improved more quickly than those who spent their days in bed."

"Really?"

"While I wouldn't recommend that you begin training for a marathon..." he smiled "...I would encourage you to walk every day, even if you only manage one turn around the block. Then gradually increase the distance.''

Laura nodded slowly. ''All right. I can do that.''

He handed her a pamphlet. ''Here's some information to study. Mind you, CFS is called a syndrome because it's a collection of symptoms and not a specific disease. If you want more facts, or if you'd like to talk to others who have this, there are several web sites on the internet that can help you. And if you have any problems, please, come back and see me.''

''Thanks, Doctor.''

''I'm sorry I don't have a magic pill for you.''

She smiled. ''You're not half as sorry as I am. I am glad, though, that at least I have a name for what I have. I was beginning to think that I *was* going crazy.''

''Being able to label your condition helps,'' he agreed. ''I think you'll be amazed at how many other people suffer from the same problem.''

He sent her on her way and met Aly coming out of an exam room. Immediately, her brilliant smile did strange things inside his chest. It shouldn't have been surprising. Each time she flashed her grin at him, he felt as if he'd received a boost of adrenalin. He was too old to be acting like an adolescent, but he couldn't stop himself.

''Have you seen—?'' she cut herself short as she stared at the woman ambling toward the exit. ''Was that Laura Meadows?''

''In the flesh.''

''Did you ever find out what her problem was?''

''I think so. Chronic fatigue syndrome.''

''No kidding. How do we treat it?''

''We don't, other than try to ease her symptoms.''

''What a shame. Still, I suppose it could be worse.''

''Yes, it could.''

"Have you checked on Joy Whitlow this afternoon?" she asked.

"A few minutes ago. Her temperature has dropped a half a degree, but otherwise there hasn't been any real change."

She frowned. "Shouldn't we see some results of her treatment by now?"

"Not necessarily. It hasn't been twenty-four hours yet."

"I'll stop on my way home and see her. Ann and Gary are probably wearing themselves out with worry."

"I'm sure."

"So what are you doing this evening?"

"You mean, if I'm lucky enough to not get called?"

"Yeah."

Gavin shrugged. "I'm behind in reading my journals."

"Drop by my house if you're bored."

"We'll see," he said, purposely sounding noncommittal, although he intended to respond to her invitation if given half a chance. Remembering her partially phrased question, he asked, "Who or what are you looking for?"

"I was looking for Oliver. Have you seen him?"

"Earlier this morning. Why?"

"I wanted to ask if—" A high-pitched whine pierced the air. "What is that?"

Gavin wondered the same thing. "It sounds like it's coming from the furnace room." He'd no sooner spoken than the noise stopped and Oliver limped out of the utility closet, his gray hair disheveled and his right cheek branded with an oily streak.

Gavin exchanged a glance with Aly and shrugged as she frowned. "What happened to you?" she asked.

"Checking out the furnace. The weather's turning colder and we'll need it before long." He glanced at Gavin. "I don't suppose you know anything about heating systems?"

Did Oliver honestly think Heating and Cooling 101 was

part of Gavin's medical curriculum? "Only how to change the air filters."

The older man's disgust was evident. "It figures. Well, tell Izzie she needs to get someone here right away. I don't want to wait until the snow flies."

Gavin distinctly felt as if he'd failed another of Oliver's tests. Personally, he didn't care, but he knew how badly Aly wanted the two of them to get along. Because she was worth the effort, he bit back a sharp retort.

Aly, however, true to form, clearly wasn't as restrained. "Gavin may not be a furnace expert, but you have to admit that he's a whiz at medical technology. Isn't that hook-up to the radiology department in Guymon absolutely fantastic? I got an X-ray report in no time."

"You can look at films yourself," Oliver said gruffly.

"Yes, but Clint Youngblood showed a hairline fracture of his wrist that I'd missed. I would have OK'd him for football practice and by the time I received the expert's opinion, he might have done irreparable damage."

Oliver grunted. "If a radiologist actually read that film, I'll eat my hat."

"Why do you say that?" Gavin asked. According to the X-ray technician, Oliver had seen patients who'd benefited from their latest improvement and been suitably impressed.

"It was too fast. I'll bet a computer scanned it and spit out a report. Probably missed something, too." With that, Oliver strode off, leaving Gavin shaking his head and Aly standing in stunned surprise.

"I didn't expect him to gush on and on," Aly said, "but he could have said something nice. You spent a lot of time implementing the system."

"I didn't do it for him," Gavin said gently. "I did it for the patients."

"But why is he so critical? If Pete had done that, Oliver

would have acted as if he'd discovered the cure for cancer.''

"Because I'm not Pete and never will be.'' Therein lay the crux of the whole matter. Oliver had wanted his son in his practice and he couldn't have him. If only Pete were able to give Gavin some advice on how to deal with his father. Unfortunately, he couldn't, and dwelling on the impossible wouldn't alter a thing.

Gavin changed the subject. "I see he's still limping. How's his toe?''

"He says its OK, but he won't let me look at it.''

He heard the concern and frustration in her voice and he wanted to pound some sense into Oliver's head on Aly's behalf. But he couldn't.

"Your uncle is an adult,'' he soothed. "I'm sure he's taking care of himself.''

"I don't think he is, which is what worries me.''

Gavin wondered what it would be like to have someone fret about *him*. "Maybe you should take him to dinner tonight. A dose of TLC might cure whatever ails him.''

"I haven't fixed a meal for him in a long time. What a great idea.'' To his surprise and delight, she stepped up and hugged him.

Enjoying the feel of her arms around his neck, he smiled. "I aim to please.''

Aly strode into ICU after seven o'clock and stopped at the nurses' desk. "How's Joy?''

The evening shift nurse handed over the chart. "Her temp is down and she's been awake off and on.''

"Good. How are her labs?''

"Her electrolytes are near normal and her white count is dropping steadily. It isn't normal yet, but it's getting closer.''

Aly walked into Joy's cubicle and spoke softly to Ann. "According to the nurse, Joy is responding."

"Isn't it wonderful?" Ann said happily.

"It is. Have you gone home at all today?"

"Gary and I traded places this afternoon so I could shower and change clothes. I have to confess that I even took a long nap."

"As long as you take care of yourself. Dr Sinclair and I don't need any extra patients." She grinned. "We can hardly keep up with the ones we have."

"If everyone gets the same VIP treatment you gave us, I can understand why."

As Aly left ICU, she wondered if Gavin was right. She often spent extra time with the people who came to her for treatment. If she continued, how *would* she juggle her medical commitments and her family responsibilities?

She quickly pushed the doubt aside. Other women managed, so would she. Deep in her thoughts, she plowed into Gavin as she rounded the corner to the lobby entrance.

He caught her by her arms to keep her from falling. "You look as if you're a million miles away."

"Sorry," she said. "I guess I was woolgathering."

"A dangerous occupation."

"Obviously. Where are you headed?"

"I thought I'd grab a sandwich from the cafeteria. I just finished with an eight-year-old kid in ER who burned his hands."

"What happened?"

"He wanted to roast marshmallows, so he built a fire in his back yard. Unfortunately, he thought it wasn't big enough, so he squirted some of his dad's charcoal starter fluid on it."

Aly gasped as she pictured the image.

"Needless to say, the yard caught fire and he burned his

hands trying to douse the flames before his parents found out. It didn't work.''

"How is he?''

"The burns were minor, but between them and the fire chief's lecture he'll think twice before he tries to toast marshmallows by himself again,'' he finished wryly. "Anyway, I'm starved. Will you join me?''

"I have a better idea. I'll stop by the deli on my way home and we can eat in private.''

"I thought you were eating with Oliver?''

"He's made other plans.'' Aly wasn't sure if he'd been telling her the truth or giving her an excuse. In any case, she'd tried.

Gavin reached into his back pocket, presumably for his billfold. "I'll buy.''

She refused. "Bring a roll of nickels instead.''

"Nickels?''

"That's right. Remember how Pete taught the two of us how to play poker? Well, I want to see if I still can.''

He chuckled. "You're on.''

At the store, Aly bought her food and begged the clerk for as many nickels as possible when giving her change. She drove home with potato salad, a loaf of French bread, a bottle of white wine, an oven-roasted chicken and three dollars' worth of nickels. If she didn't have enough of the five-cent pieces, no problem. She could surely negotiate some other form of payment.

Being rusty, her small stash of coins dwindled quite quickly, but she didn't mind. Spending time with Gavin was worth every nickel she lost, especially when he suggested that she pay her IOUs in kisses. Her first financial installment would have lasted the rest of the evening if not for an urgent summons to the ER.

"I have to go,'' he said reluctantly.

"I understand," she replied, equally as disappointed. "There will be other evenings."

"Count on it."

And so began their new routine. After work, Aly would either meet Gavin for dinner at the hospital cafeteria or would invite him over to her house. Occasionally he would reciprocate, although he admitted that his culinary skills left a lot to be desired.

Aly didn't care if he served shoe leather. His company meant far more to her than anything else.

As September drew to a close, she knew with growing certainty that Gavin was the only man for her. They shared so much, from their personal interests to their vision for the community. He'd even come out of his shell and had agreed to help build the hospital's float for the annual Fall Festival's opening parade which, barring inclement weather, was always held on the first weekend of October. The staff had embraced his idea of turning the plain trailer skirting into an EKG strip and so his and Aly's job had been to design the characteristic blip pattern. They'd poked hundreds of squares of red tissue paper into the chicken-wire framework that hid the trailer's wheels and used thousands more pieces of white as the background.

Even if they didn't win the prize, the hours spent with Gavin were ample enough reward, as far as Aly was concerned.

Although their personal relationship was rolling along the right track, the relationship between Oliver and Gavin remained rocky. No matter what Gavin did, Oliver's attitude toward him didn't soften. During her make-up dinner date with her uncle, she'd tried to talk to him, but he'd refused to discuss Gavin at all. "I don't want to ruin my appetite," he'd said.

Fortunately, no one seemed to notice the strain between

the two physicians. At least, if they did, they understood the reasons and therefore didn't comment.

Oliver's actions, however, drove Aly to her wits' end. Although Gavin claimed that being ignored didn't bother him, she suspected otherwise. She'd spent enough time with him to recognize the signs. There were evenings he would jog a few extra miles or insist on staying home alone to catch up on his reading.

On the other nights, they didn't have any trouble occupying the hours. No matter what they did, they usually ended their time together in far more pleasurable activities.

All in all, their romance sailed along at a steady clip. Aly hadn't realized just how successful she'd been at convincing him they were meant for each other until Gavin pulled her close one evening.

"You're the only woman I've ever wanted," he told her.

She smiled. "Music to my ears."

"If I could, I'd marry you in a heartbeat."

Her happiness dimmed. "Who said you can't?" she asked lightly.

"Your uncle won't stand for it. He'll do his best to tear us apart."

After weeks of seeing Oliver's unyielding attitude, Aly reluctantly accepted the fact, yet she had to be optimistic. "What can he do? He doesn't have any leverage. Everything I have is mine and he can't fire me. So, you see, his hands are tied."

"He'll think of something."

"Maybe he will and maybe he won't. How long are you willing to put our future on hold?"

He held her close. "I don't know."

At least he was honest. Their relationship had progressed quickly, which in her eyes indicated that it had been decreed by fate. However, Gavin didn't have the same inner assurance and until he did, they would need to wait.

Perhaps if Gavin only had Oliver to contend with, he would be more willing to gamble. Although she'd done her best to show her support and stand by him, she wasn't sure she had done enough to convince him of her loyalty. Adding that doubt to his dysfunctional family history, she understood why he hesitated.

"OK," she said against his chest. "We'll play by your rules. In the meantime, we'll just love each other. When you're ready, I'll be here."

It was less than ideal, but for now it would have to be enough.

"I suppose you're spending your weekend at the Fall Festival?" Izzie asked at noon on the following Friday.

"Where else would I be?" Aly asked.

Izzie shrugged. "Oh, I'd think you'd take advantage of all the commotion so you and Dr Sinclair could disappear for a few days."

Aly smiled. Keeping her feelings for Gavin hidden from Izzie's view had been impossible. Although Aly wouldn't advertise their relationship, she didn't intend to behave as if she were ashamed of it either. If Oliver didn't say or do anything to interfere, she could effectively deflate Gavin's objections to a wedding.

"I thought about getting away, but with the extra people in town our services might be needed." She grinned. "Besides, are we acting obvious?"

Izzie snorted. "Just because you don't hold hands or coo over each other like teenagers doesn't mean folks can't tell something's brewing between the two of you. Anyone with half a brain and mediocre eyesight can figure it out."

"Has anyone said anything?"

"I've heard some speculation, but only from a few. Personally, I think most would feel better knowing how you two feel about each other. They want to make sure our newest doc doesn't up and leave. A wedding would go a long way to make people confident that he'll stick around for the next thirty years or so.''

"Gavin thinks Oliver will interfere if we make an announcement.''

"He probably will. Why your uncle can't let go of the past and move on is beyond me. Everyone knows that the young doc is no more responsible for Pete's death than I am.''

"I wish I could get through to him,'' Aly fretted. "I thought he'd change his mind once he got to know Gavin, but he hasn't.''

"I hate to say this, but it may come down to you making a choice.''

Aly sighed. Izzie's comment seemed ominous, and was far more depressing than Aly wanted to consider. However, the next phone call drove the subject completely out of her mind.

"Hedda Peabody was just in an accident,'' Izzie reported. "ER says it's our turn to cover and wants one of you to check her out. They're only reporting minor injuries.''

"Then I'll go,'' Aly decided.

"Do you want me to send Dr Sinclair over?''

She hesitated. Gavin was trying to finish his appointments before they reported to the park where the hospital's float had been towed for the start of the parade. "Let me assess her first. Tell him where I went, though, in case I need him.''

Within ten minutes, she was standing in Hedda's cubicle, noticing how frail the elderly woman appeared in the hospital bed. She was pale and her age-spotted hands shook as she tried to restore the fine strands of hair to her bun.

"How are you doing, Miss Peabody?'' Aly asked, aware of the police officer waiting outside.

"I've certainly felt better. It isn't every day a person gets run down crossing the street."

The ER nurse had noted bruising and contusions on Hedda's right leg, so Aly raised the covers to examine the damage. Sure enough, a bruise the size of a fist had formed on her upper thigh and a pale purple knot the size of a peach pit was on her shin. Various scrapes and smaller bruises dotted both extremities below her knees.

"Did the car hit you?"

"I don't know if the driver actually hit me or if I fell against the car as he squealed to a stop. The curb seems to have done the worst damage."

Her explanation accounted for the knot, which was well below the range of a car's bumper. "How are you feeling otherwise?"

"Shaky. I'll be fine if I can just rest a few minutes."

"Rest is the best thing for you," Aly agreed. "I'm going to check you over, though, just to make sure everything else is fine. Did you hit your head?"

"No."

Aly ran through the usual checks of pupil response, heart and lungs, and palpated her abdomen. By the time she'd finished, Hedda was exhausted.

"I haven't had such a thorough exam in years."

"We want you to get your money's worth," Aly said with a smile. "As far as I can tell, other than the bruises, you're in excellent shape."

"Then I can go home?"

Hedda's unsteadiness wasn't particularly worrisome. Anyone would have shaken like a leaf if they'd come as close as Hedda had to the afterlife. However, because the elderly librarian lived alone and had no family to check on her, Aly hated to send her on her way so quickly.

"I'd rather you stay a few hours so the nurse can keep an eye on you," Aly said. "I'm sure she can round up a cup of coffee or tea to settle your nerves. Then, after you take a catnap and are feeling more like yourself, we'll find someone to drive you home.''

Hedda smiled a tired smile. ''Thank you, dear. I'd like that.''

Aly patted her hand. ''Just relax, and if you have any problems, the nurse will contact me.''

Hedda nodded and closed her eyes. Aly left to speak to the nurse. ''Give her a cup of hot tea and let her rest. If she wakes up perky, she's free to go. Otherwise, you can reach me on my cellphone.''

The nurse nodded. ''Going to the parade?''

''After putting in all that hard work on our float, I wouldn't miss it.''

Aly spoke to the officer, assured him that Miss Peabody would be OK, then returned to her office, where she met Gavin at the door.

''I just finished and was on my way to the hospital,'' he said. ''What's the scoop?''

''Bumps and bruises. She'll be fine.''

''Then let's go.''

''You're in a quite a hurry,'' she said as she lengthened her stride to keep up with his.

He slowed his pace and grinned sheepishly. ''I don't want to be late. I've never been part of a parade before.''

''You haven't?''

He shook his head. ''According to my father, Sinclairs don't participate in such bourgeois activities.''

''Not even for your high-school homecoming?''

''Not even then,'' he said firmly.

She threaded one arm through his. ''Then we're going to complete your education.''

An hour later, sitting on the float's hospital bed with Gavin standing beside her, she honestly felt as if she hadn't ever been so happy. Smiling at the crowd required absolutely no effort on her part. As she waved at everyone on the sidelines and threw wrapped candy pieces at the children in the street, she realized how much she'd missed during these past few years because of her grueling schedule. Launching Gavin into the community's social events had also helped her to take on a more active role and boosted her enthusiasm.

Her cheerfulness dimmed some five minutes later when she glimpsed Oliver standing next to her mother in the crowd. He raised one eyebrow as if to ask who was minding their office before he pointedly looked away.

He wouldn't ruin this day for her, she told herself firmly. If he wanted to be miserable, he could. Izzie had agreed to man the phones and keep their clinic doors open. In case of an emergency, both she and Gavin were a phone call away.

Thirty minutes later, the parade had completed its loop and they were back at the park where they'd started. Aly was still sitting on the hospital bed, talking to her cohorts, when her cellphone trilled.

"It's Hedda Peabody," the ER nurse told her.

"What's wrong?" Her slight hesitation gave Aly the briefest of warnings.

"She's dead."

CHAPTER TEN

ALY listened incredulously. "She's *what*?"

"You'd better get here," the nurse said, sounding as shocked as Aly felt.

"I'm on my way." Aly snapped the phone closed. If Hedda had indeed died, rushing wouldn't help her. Aly, however, simply couldn't wait. She nudged Gavin as she slid off the hospital bed.

"ER called. We have to go."

He didn't argue. Instead, he vaulted over the side and landed lightly on his feet. Once on the ground, he held out his hands to catch her as she, too, jumped off the trailer.

The crowd parted, clearly understanding the reasons for their hurried departure without being told. Gavin pushed his way through the people lining the sidewalk and Aly gratefully followed in his wake. As soon as they could talk relatively privately, he asked, "What happened?"

"Hedda died."

"She died? Are they doing CPR?"

"I don't know."

"I thought she only had bumps and bruises."

Nausea gripped Aly's stomach. "That's all I found. I feel terrible. What if I missed something?" She shook her head. "Obviously I did, but I can't believe how I could have possibly let something serious slip by. All her readings were normal."

"Don't second-guess yourself," Gavin advised as they reached his SUV. It seemed pointless to take her car too, so she piled into the passenger's side. "We'll know more after we talk to the staff."

170

Aly couldn't follow his advice. Instead, she mentally replayed every moment, every clinical observation from the moment that she'd first seen Hedda to the last. What had she ignored? Overlooked? Or, God forbid, simply dismissed?

She hadn't arrived at any answers by the time Gavin pulled into the ER's driveway. Before he'd stopped the engine, she bolted out and darted through the automatic doors.

"What happened?" Aly demanded of the same ER nurse she'd seen earlier.

"It was so unexpected, and so peaceful," the nurse began. "After Hedda drank her tea, she said she was tired. I dimmed the lights so she could rest. I peeked in on her fifteen minutes later and she appeared to be sleeping so I didn't disturb her. When I came back fifteen minutes after that, something didn't seem quite right so I went in and immediately saw that she wasn't breathing."

"You never checked her vitals during that time?" Gavin asked, obviously arriving in time to hear her report.

"I didn't have any orders to," she defended. "Only to let her rest, and when she felt stronger to let her leave."

"Did she complain of chest pain at any time?" Gavin questioned. "Shortness of breath? Headache?"

The nurse shook her head. "Nothing. She only wanted to take a nap."

Aly remembered discussing those same symptoms with her patient. Hedda had emphatically denied any such problems.

"Did she have a history of heart disease or clotting problems?"

Aly seized on his last suggestion. "Do you think she suffered a pulmonary embolism? She had a huge knot on her leg from falling."

"It's possible. It's also possible that her heart simply gave out. Did you try CPR?"

"Yes, but as soon as Dr Crawford walked in he took one look at her and said it was too late."

"Why weren't we called sooner?"

"I asked my clerk to locate you, but she notified Dr Crawford instead because he's scheduled as the covering physician," she said. "I didn't realize until later that she hadn't contacted you at all. I thought you'd want to know because she came in as your patient."

As if on cue, Oliver came out of the trauma cubicle. "The parade must be over."

His implication stung. "We came as soon as we heard," Aly said. "I can't imagine what went wrong. She was fine when I left. A little shaky from her experience with the car, but that was all."

"Something obviously wasn't right." Oliver sat behind the desk with her chart. "She was remarkably healthy for a woman in her seventies."

Oliver's dry tone only served to intensify Aly's feelings of guilt. Perhaps she should have hung around, but Hedda's injuries had seemed so mild.

"Do you know if she had any cardiac problems?" Gavin asked.

Oliver sighed. "None. She was very conscious of heart disease. She walked, sipped a jigger-full of wine as her daily constitutional, took a low dose of aspirin every morning for the last fifteen years and worried over her cholesterol."

"That doesn't mean she couldn't have suffered a massive infarct," Gavin pointed out.

"True, but she did suffer a leg injury and could easily have formed a deep vein thrombosis," Oliver insisted. "She may have thrown a pulmonary embolism, which was a possibility Aly should have considered."

"I'm sure she would have if Hedda had exhibited other signs, like labored breathing, cyanosis and chest pain, to name a few."

Oliver ignored Gavin to speak directly to Aly. "If she wasn't able to go home, you should have requested closer nursing care. More importantly, you should have stayed longer and observed her yourself. It wouldn't surprise me if her death could have been avoided."

"You don't know that," Gavin insisted. "There are too many unknowns here."

After all the times Aly had rushed to Gavin's defense, it seemed strange to be on the receiving end. Hearing her uncle, who'd always been so supportive, so encouraging and so inspiring, find fault with her in such a belligerent manner was deeply unsettling.

She gave a wavering sigh. "If we want answers, we have to request an autopsy." The thought of having made a mistake haunted her.

"I've already arranged for a post-mortem." Oliver turned to the nurse. "Move the body to the morgue. The funeral home will pick it up later."

The nurse left to handle the necessary chores, clearly subdued by the day's events. Most likely she, too, had felt Oliver's wrath.

Aly met her uncle's gaze. "You think I screwed up, don't you?"

Oliver glanced at Gavin before he met her gaze. "I think your mind isn't on your work any more."

"How can you say that?" she demanded.

Oliver snorted. "I know what you two are doing in your spare time. I wasn't born yesterday and, even if I had been, people talk."

"What's wrong with Aly and I seeing each other?" Gavin asked, his voice cold.

"You're distracting her. She's not staying focused."

A muscle tensed in Gavin's jaw. ''Then you're saying I'm at fault?''

''If the shoe fits.''

Aly was appalled. It was as if Gavin's fears were being realized before her very eyes. ''How can you say that? *I* was the one who saw the patient.''

''Yes, you were,'' Oliver agreed. ''Maybe if you hadn't been in such a hurry to meet Sinclair, you would have spared a few more minutes for Hedda.''

''I wasn't in a hurry,'' she protested. ''I was eager to get to the parade, I'll admit, but I examined her thoroughly. She didn't complain about anything other than her sore leg.''

''The body headed to the morgue suggests otherwise.''

Gavin spoke up. ''You're drawing conclusions without any facts. Number one, we don't know why Hedda died and to accuse Aly of being distracted is premature. The woman may have simply suffered a massive heart attack and if a cardiologist had stood by, he couldn't have reversed the damage.

''Number two, Aly has never let her personal life interfere with her professional duties. If she thought Hedda required medical attention, you can bet that she would have skipped the parade entirely. And if she'd called me, I would have, too.''

''The point is,'' Oliver snapped, ''she would never have gotten caught up in this parade business in the first place if not for you.''

''So now she can't become involved in community events?'' Gavin asked. ''I'm surprised you don't expect her to live at the hospital.''

The entire situation had gotten out of hand and Aly couldn't deal with it. Losing Hedda was enough of a blow. She couldn't stand to see the two men in her life in conflict as well.

"Stop it, both of you," she cried. "This has got to end."

Oliver nodded his head. "You're right. It does. You're going to have to choose between him…" he pointed in Gavin's direction "…or your profession."

Aly's mind reeled under his directive. Was Oliver right? Had her mind been elsewhere? Had she, even subconsciously, been more interested in joining Gavin than in paying attention to her patient?

"Don't listen to him, Aly," Gavin ordered. "He's wrong about everything."

Oliver raised an eyebrow. "Am I?"

"Come on, Aly," Gavin said. "We've heard enough. I'll take you home."

As much as she wanted to follow him to the door, leaving would only postpone the inevitable. She shook her head. "I'm staying. You go on."

He froze. "You're staying? What for?"

"Oliver and I have a few things to discuss."

This time he pulled her into the supply room for privacy. "Don't you see? Oliver is playing on your guilt to force you to choose between us."

It was crystal clear. In days past, when the sheer volume of patients had provided more of a distraction than Gavin ever had, Oliver hadn't made such ridiculous accusations or demands.

"I know."

"Then why are you letting him?"

"I'm not letting him do anything. I need to figure out for myself what went wrong and I have to do that here."

"Listen to me, Aly. Some people can't be saved. At seventy-eight, Hedda had lived a full life. If anything had seemed out of the ordinary, you would have intervened. I trust your judgement. You were—*are*—thorough."

She managed a tight smile. "In my heart, I believe that, but I still have my doubts. Oliver is right, though. I should have stayed another fifteen minutes. We stayed all night with Joy and she recovered.''

''Joy recovered because she received massive doses of antibiotics in the nick of time. It had nothing to do with whether we were there to watch the IV drip or not,'' he insisted. ''Our presence isn't magical.''

''I know. I just wonder if I am trying to do too much. I want it all—you know, a career, a family—but some people simply can't have everything they want.''

''No one gets everything they want. You may have to scale down your professional duties, but there isn't any reason why you can't have a family and a career.'' He fell silent for a moment. ''If you'll put aside your emotions and look at this objectively, you'll see that this isn't about Hedda. It's about your uncle exerting control over your life. He doesn't want me in Pete's place and he won't stop until I'm gone.''

The truth was undeniable. She sighed, disappointed that she'd failed to bring Gavin and her uncle to common ground. If only she could break through her uncle's anger.

''There is a solution,'' he said slowly.

She hadn't seen one, but if Gavin had—what a wondrous thought. ''What?''

''This isn't the only town where the people need a doctor and a nurse-practitioner.''

Leave Hartwell? As far as she was concerned, it wasn't a solution. ''I can't leave.''

''Why not?''

''What would my patients and my family do? They need me.''

''I need you, too.''

Suddenly the love and loyalty for her family stood as an opposing force to her love and loyalty for Gavin. ''You're not being fair,'' she told him. ''You're doing the same thing to me that Oliver is trying to do—demanding that I choose between you. Well, I can't do it. I won't.''

Gavin's face suddenly seemed as if it were carved in stone. ''You're wrong, Alison. Whether you opt to stay or to go, you're making a decision. In this case, there is no middle ground. As someone once told me, 'Choose the option you can live with'.''

Gavin drove toward the Crawford Medical Practice building, well aware that there was more at stake than simply knowing the exact cause of Hedda's death. As he'd already pointed out, Oliver was only trying to manipulate Aly into falling in line with his wishes. Most physicians would have waited for the pathology report before correcting a problem that didn't exist. Not Oliver. As far as the older physician was concerned, Gavin was the problem, plain and simple.

Hedda's demise had hit Aly hard, but he couldn't imagine her relinquishing her practice because of it. She dispensed as many smiles as medicine, and her optimism and cheerfulness were equally as powerful.

He'd hoped she would accept his suggestion to build a practice elsewhere without any hesitation, but his long shot hadn't paid off. She'd only sought him out in the first place because of her concern for her patients. Her fierce loyalty to them was admirable, but he hadn't realized how firmly those ties bound her. Obviously, her love for him wasn't as strong and secure, which was what Oliver was counting on. Even if by some miracle she agreed to go with him, her heart would always be here. That wasn't what he wanted either.

If he left—alone—Aly would be free to do what she did best…look after her friends and family. Given enough time, she could find another doctor to take his place.

As he walked into the building, the thought nearly drove him to his knees. He didn't want to go—he'd only accomplished a fraction of what he and Pete had planned—but he loved Aly too much to put her through this every time a tragedy struck. From his viewpoint, *he* was one who needed to make a decision about staying or going, and his choice was clear.

He wrote his resignation letter and sealed it in an envelope addressed to Oliver. His last act before he left would be to deliver it into the older man's hands.

A few minutes later, he approached Izzie. "I need the number for the locum service."

Izzie immediately scrawled it on a piece of paper. "Who's planning to be gone?"

"I am." Forgoing further explanations, he returned to his office and made his call. He might not be here, but at least he wouldn't leave Aly to pick up the pieces by herself.

The first thing Alison noticed as she drove into her usual parking spot at their medical office was that Oliver's car was at the far end and Gavin's was missing. The peace she'd discovered at the hospital as she'd realized that she'd done everything humanly possible for Hedda suddenly disappeared. Her instincts immediately screamed a warning and she rushed inside to corner Izzie.

"Where's Gavin?" she asked breathlessly.

"He left."

"When?"

"Ten, fifteen minutes."

Stay calm, she told herself. "Where did he go?"

Izzie shrugged. "He just said goodbye. Of course, that was after I gave him the phone number of the locum service."

"He asked for the phone number?"

"Yeah, but he didn't say why he needed it."

Aly pinched the bridge of her nose and swallowed the rapidly appearing lump in her throat. "He's gone."

"That's what I just said."

"No. I mean, he's gone. For good," she explained dully.

"After what we went through, don't be joking with me, girl."

"It's true." Aly explained everything, including how she'd told Gavin to leave without her. She finished with, "It's like reliving that day three years ago. Actually, it's worse, because I love him so much." The pain in her chest came from her heart breaking in two. The coming years seemed dark and dreary and stretched ahead like an eternity.

"I can see that."

"I was going to tell him how I felt once I got here, but I'm too late."

"Where would he go?"

"I don't have a clue. Oklahoma City, I guess." Last time she'd known where to find him and had drawn comfort from that knowledge. Now she wouldn't have the faintest idea of where to look.

Aly numbly moved into her office and sank into a chair. "He left because of Oliver, you know."

"I'm not surprised. Your uncle didn't treat him like he should have," Izzie stated vehemently.

Anger began to build inside Aly. "To think I've spent my days trying to make his life easier and this is what happens."

"Well, girl, you never asked my opinion, but now I'm giving it to you. You haven't done Oliver any favors by knocking yourself out. He doesn't have any idea what you've given up or what you *are* giving up because of him."

Izzie was right. Aly had shielded her uncle from so many things in order to spare him any worries and aggravation. If Oliver had lived through what she had these past two years, he'd beg Gavin to stay.

The prospect of never seeing Gavin again was too horrible to think about. "He's probably at home, packing," she thought aloud, "So call my mother and ask her to do whatever it takes to keep Gavin from leaving before I get there."

Izzie's face shone with excitement. "Now you're talking."

"I'll be in Oliver's office. This time I'm not going to dance around the issues to spare his feelings."

"Good girl!"

Aly strode into his office without knocking. "Gavin left."

Her uncle shrugged as he waved a sheet of paper. "His resignation was under my door. I knew he wouldn't last."

"Because you always intended to run him off."

"That's not true," he said without conviction.

She leaned over his desk and planted both hands on the top. "Isn't it? You never accepted him. Even when he brought about a lot of changes for the better, you never encouraged or praised him." She straightened. "If Pete were here, he wouldn't be happy with the way you've treated his friend."

Oliver fell silent and she continued. "No matter what I do or how much I take on, you refuse to take care of yourself. If you want to run this practice into the ground, go ahead. You have Gavin's resignation. I'm giving you mine, effective immediately."

"You can't quit," he roared, half rising out of his chair.

"I just did."

Oliver sank down as if he'd lost all of his stuffing. "I need you here."

"You needed Gavin more."

"We're partners. You can't just leave."

"I hate to tell you this, but Gavin has been more than an employee. He's been your partner all along."

Oliver scoffed. "That's impossible. I didn't sign anything over to him—" He cut himself off. "You sold him your shares, didn't you?"

Aly shook her head. "I *gave* them to him."

"How could you?" Oliver's voice broke. "Those were Pete's."

She skirted the desk to perch on the front edge near him. "Yes, they were, but you passed them to me because Pete wasn't here. I transferred them to Gavin because I thought he would look after them wisely."

"And now he's leaving," Oliver snarled.

Aly held onto her temper. "I don't have the time or the inclination to argue with you. I will tell you one thing, though. Gavin came to Hartwell, not because I begged him to or because you needed help. He came because he wanted to see Pete's dream fulfilled. Quite a fitting memorial, wouldn't you say?"

Oliver swiveled his chair and stared out the window. "People already sing Sinclair's praises. They've forgotten my son."

Suddenly she understood why his animosity had grown after Gavin had implemented the new X-ray procedures. "No, they haven't," she assured him. "Everyone knows Gavin moved here because of his friendship with Pete. Gavin had mentioned how Pete had wanted a diagnostic wing at the hospital. Guess who he wanted to name it after?"

A light suddenly flared in Oliver's eyes. "Pete?"

"None other."

Plainly surprised by the news, Oliver fell silent. "He never said," he finally said.

"If you'd ever talked to him like an equal, you might have discovered his plans for yourself. I also wouldn't be surprised if he'd intended to establish a scholarship in

Pete's name for local students to study medicine. So, you see, Gavin won't let Pete be forgotten."

She rose. "Unfortunately, I don't expect his replacement to be as considerate. Now, if you'll excuse me, I have things to do and people to see."

"Where will you go?"

"Wherever Gavin decides to live will be fine with me." She walked toward the doorway.

"Do you love him?"

Oliver's quiet question stopped her in her tracks. She turned and smiled. "More than you can possibly imagine."

Aly rushed past a startled Izzie and hurried to her car. She flew home, praying that her mother had kept Gavin at the house until she arrived.

After she pulled her mother's painting off the wall of her bedroom, she dashed out to her car once again. "Let him be there," she begged aloud as she spun around corners and dodged traffic with the finesse of a racing driver.

Gavin's SUV was parked on the street. Sending up a silent prayer of thanks, she grabbed the canvas and hurried up the walk.

Maggie met her at the door. "He's upstairs."

"Thanks, Mom."

"What's going on?"

"I'll tell you later."

Aly forced herself to climb the steps at a sedate pace. On the landing, she knocked on the connecting door between her mother's part of the house and the rental apartment. A heavy tread and the jangle of the chain being removed gave her an extra few seconds to compose herself before Gavin opened the door.

"What are you doing here?" he asked, frowning.

"You left me again."

"There didn't seem any point in staying."

"Actually, there was." She thrust the canvas at him. "I

came to show you the painting that will hang in our future office.''

"Our future office?'' he repeated.

"I'm going wherever you go. If you'd stayed longer, you would have found that out. Unless, of course, you're rescinding your offer.''

"I'm not, but are you sure that this is what you want to do?'' he asked cautiously.

"I'm positive.'' She motioned past him. "Can we discuss this inside?''

He let her pass, then followed her in. "What about your family? Your patients?''

"Oliver will manage with a locum until he finds someone permanent.''

"And you're OK with that?''

"He made his choice,'' she said simply as she placed the canvas on the sofa, leaning it against the back cushions. "I'm making mine. You see, I took your advice and made the choice I could live with. I love you, Gavin, and I knew I couldn't bear for us to be separated again.''

Before she knew what had happened, he'd pulled her close. "I love you, too, Alison. I didn't want to leave any more than I did the first time, but I can't fight Oliver at every turn.''

"I don't want you to either. I'd rather you save your energy for other things.''

She pulled his head close, but the instant her lips touched his Gavin took control. His arms snaked around her waist and his kiss became possessive. "I agree,'' he mumbled.

She wanted this moment to last for ever, but if they didn't stop now, they wouldn't until tomorrow. Somehow she didn't think her mother would wait that long to learn what was going on. Besides, she would prefer the privacy of her own apartment for celebrating their love and commitment to each other. Perhaps Gavin thought the same, because he broke away.

"I can't believe this is happening. Ten minutes ago everything seemed bleak, and now my life seems too good to be true."

"Sometimes situations fall into place and sometimes they don't. It was our turn for a miracle," she said simply.

Clearly uncertain, he gazed at the canvas. "How did you know how much I liked this painting?"

She smiled. "It's been my favorite, too. You see, I look at that scene and see hope."

Gavin studied it from several angles. "You do?"

"Sure." She pointed to the clump of wildflowers growing near the base of the abandoned barn. "These sturdy little flowers may get battered and beaten, but they come back year after year."

"They do, don't they?" he mused. Yet he couldn't help but realize how wild things survived better in their natural environment. Would Aly grow and flourish in different surroundings? Before he could answer his own question, she continued.

"Now all we need is an office to hang it in."

Oliver's familiar voice came from the open doorway. "I know where two are available."

Gavin stared at the older man in surprise. "Pardon me?"

Oliver stepped over the threshold. "I didn't intend to barge in, but the door was open. I'd like you both to stay."

Gavin and Aly exchanged glances. "Give us one good reason why," he said bluntly.

Color tinged Oliver's cheekbones. "I'll give you two. First of all, the pathologist called. He was going out of town this weekend and went ahead and did the post-mortem on Hedda right away. The valves in her heart literally exploded. There was nothing anyone could have done.

"Second, and most importantly, Aly forced me to face

a few hard truths this afternoon, and after she finished, Izzie gave me her two cents' worth. I came to explain and beg your pardon.

"I was angry at Pete for dying prematurely, and because he wasn't around to blame I took it out on you. I was also jealous that you were doing the things Pete had wanted to do, getting the credit that Pete would have gotten, and I hated you for enjoying the spotlight when my son…" His voice cracked. "My son couldn't."

"I was only doing what Pete and I had set out to accomplish together," Gavin said.

"Aly pointed that out to me," Oliver said quietly. "Anyway, I'm sorry, and I'd like you to reconsider your decision. We can always use a good physician in town."

The sudden turn of events made it seem to Gavin as if he were living a dream. It had taken a great deal of courage and humility to apologize and he respected Oliver for his effort.

"I also know from personal experience that Hartwell is a wonderful place to raise a family," Oliver continued.

Gavin glanced at Aly and she answered his silent query. "The choice is yours."

How could he leave when this was the place they both wanted to be? "We'll stay."

Oliver's mouth trembled and the tension wrinkles across his forehead eased. "Good. I'll leave you two kids alone to work out the rest of your plans. I presume we'll celebrate a wedding soon?"

Gavin slid his arm around Aly's waist. "Yes."

"Before the snow flies," Aly promised.

Gavin pulled her close, vaguely aware of Oliver's departure. "We have to wait that long?"

Her smile shone like the sun. "We could always fly to Reno. Keep in mind, however, that you'll face a lot of unhappy people, including my uncle, if they don't watch us tie the knot.''

"You're right. I'd hate to fall out of his good graces when I've only been in them a few minutes.''

"A wise decision.''

He nuzzled her ear. "Snow season is months away, though.''

She giggled. "I've seen flurries in November. Do you think you can hold out until then?''

"It'll be tough, but I suppose I can manage.''

"Hey, I just remembered,'' she said. "Pete's birthday was November second. Shall we share our day with him?''

Touched by her thoughtfulness, Gavin smiled down at his future bride. "Considering how he brought us together, not once but twice, I'd say that date is extremely appropriate.''

He bent his head to kiss her as one thought ran through his mind.

Thank you, Pete.

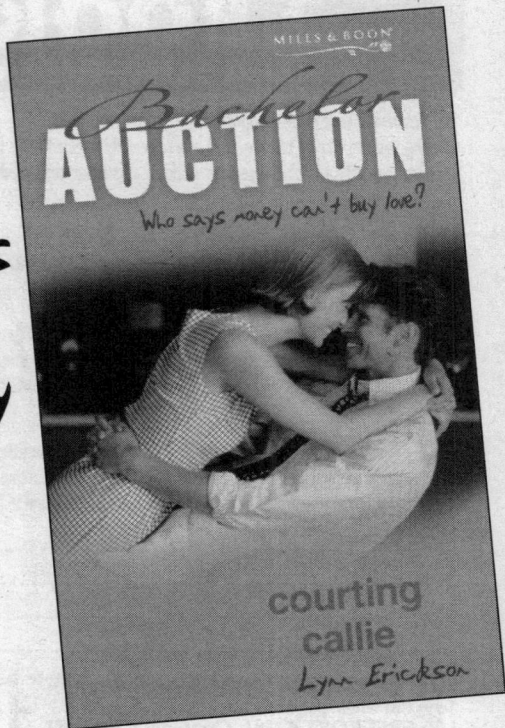

FREE

2 BOOKS
AND A SURPRISE GIFT!

We would like to take this opportunity to thank you for reading this Mills & Boon® book by offering you the chance to take TWO more specially selected titles from the Medical Romance™ series absolutely FREE! We're also making this offer to introduce you to the benefits of the Reader Service™ —

- ★ FREE home delivery
- ★ FREE monthly Newsletter
- ★ FREE gifts and competitions
- ★ Exclusive Reader Service discount
- ★ Books available before they're in the shops

Accepting these FREE books and gift places you under no obligation to buy; you may cancel at any time, even after receiving your free shipment. Simply complete your details below and return the entire page to the address below. *You don't even need a stamp!*

YES! Please send me 2 free Medical Romance books and a surprise gift. I understand that unless you hear from me, I will receive 4 superb new titles every month for just £2.55 each, postage and packing free. I am under no obligation to purchase any books and may cancel my subscription at any time. The free books and gift will be mine to keep in any case.

M2ZEC

Ms/Mrs/Miss/Mr ....Initials ....
BLOCK CAPITALS PLEASE

Surname ....

Address ....

....

....Postcode ....

Send this whole page to:
UK: FREEPOST CN81, Croydon, CR9 3WZ
EIRE: PO Box 4546, Kilcock, County Kildare (stamp required)